The NODDY Treasury

Text copyright © 1984 Darrell Waters Limited
Illustrations copyright © 1984 Macdonald & Co
(Publishers) Limited
Published 1984 by Purnell Books
A Division of Macdonald & Co (Publishers) Ltd,
3rd Floor, Greater London House,
Hampstead Road, London NW1
a member of Maxwell Pergamon Publishing Corporation plc
Reprinted 1988

Material first published in Noddy Big Books
1952 to 1974, Noddy's Own Nursery Rhymes 1958
and Noddy Ark series
ISBN 0-361-06066-1
Printed in Great Britain by Purnell Book
Production Limited, a member of BPCC

Purnell

Contents

NODDY HAS A FUNNY IDEA

ONE day when Noddy drove up to the Toadstool House to call on his friend Big-Ears, he had a great surprise. Big-Ears was packing his suit-case to go away!

"Oh Big-Ears," said Noddy, "you didn't tell me you were going away! Where are you going?"

"My brother Little-Ears wants me," said Big-Ears. "He's going to paint his house and I said I would go and help him."

"I'll come too," said Noddy. "I'd like to paint a house—splish-splash-splish-splash!"

"I daresay you would," said Big-Ears. "But Little-Ears doesn't want you, Noddy. Don't you remember—last time you went there, he asked you to weed his garden—and you pulled up all his seedlings."

"Well—they *looked* like weeds," said Noddy. "All right. I won't come. But I shall miss you, Big-Ears. Are you going to take your cat with you?"

"No, I can't," said Big-Ears. "The smell of new paint makes him sick. I wondered if Mr. Plod would look after him for me."

"Mr. Plod! But he doesn't *like* cats," said Noddy.

"No—*I'll* look after your old cat for you, Big-Ears."

"He'd never stay with you!" said Big-Ears. "He hardly ever *looks* at you."

"He *is* rather a stand-offish cat," said Noddy, nodding his head. "But I know how to keep him close to me ALL the time, Big-Ears."

"You don't," said Big-Ears. "He won't come near you! And he'd run away from your house as soon as you took him there."

"He wouldn't," said Noddy. "I'll just show you. Wait here a minute, Big-Ears."

Noddy ran out to his little car. He had his shopping there, and in one parcel was some fish for his dinner. Noddy did a MOST peculiar thing with it! He unwrapped it from its paper, put the fish down on the grass—and wiped his feet on it! Yes— he really did. He wiped them and wiped them. Then he cut the piece of fish in half —and put a piece into each of his pockets!

Then he went back to Big-Ears' house. "Puss, Puss, Puss!" he called.

To Big-Ears' surprise the cat ran round Noddy, purring loudly, and rubbed its head against Noddy's

feet. "Now—you come with me, cat," said Noddy. "Keep close to me and don't run away. Come along!"

And the cat kept close to Noddy and went purring with him to the car! Big-Ears went to the gate in astonishment.

"Noddy! Why does my cat suddenly follow you like that?" he called. "Is it a spell?"

"Well—a *kind* of spell!" shouted back Noddy, as the cat settled comfortably beside him in his car. "Have a good time, Big-Ears. I promise you that your cat will never leave me as long as you are away!"

Well, well! Big-Ears was really very, very puzzled. His old cat had NEVER behaved with anyone in such a way before. Certainly not with Noddy! He finished his packing, got on his bicycle, and rode off to Little-Ears' house, still feeling surprised.

Mr. and Mrs. Tubby Bear were surprised too, when they saw how Big-Ears' cat followed Noddy about everywhere. "Why he might be *your* cat," said Mrs. Tubby.

"He never leaves you, Noddy! He's always rubbing against your legs and purring. He must be very, very fond of you!"

Big-Ears came back in two days' time and went to Noddy's house to collect his cat. "I wonder if my old cat is still purring round Noddy," he thought. "I'm sure he's not! He's either run away back to my house—or Noddy has had to keep him shut up somewhere."

Noddy was outside, cleaning his car. Big-Ears saw him there—and saw the cat too. Goodness gracious—it was actually lying down on Noddy's feet! When Noddy moved, the cat jumped off, followed him round, rubbing its head against him and purring all the time. Big-Ears couldn't understand it. Why, his cat had never loved *him* like that!

"Hey, Noddy!" he called. "I'm back—and I see my cat is still loving you. What is this wonderful cat-spell you've got? Do tell me!"

"Well, if you like, I'll get a bit of the spell and rub it on *you*!" said Noddy, with a laugh. "Wait there, Big-Ears."

He hurried indoors and fetched a bit of fish. "Shut your eyes!" he called as he came out with it—and then he rubbed it over Big-Ears' shoes.

"Now walk out of the gate and your cat will come at once!" he said. And, of course, as soon as Big-Ears walked away, the cat, smelling the fresh fish, ran after him at once.

"Wonderful!" said Big-Ears. "I'll buy the secret of that spell from you, Noddy. Look—here's five pence for it!"

"All right!" said Noddy. "I just rubbed some fish on your boots. Ha ha! That's all it was—and you gave me five pence for that! Let's go and spend it at the ice-cream shop—but first I'll change my shoes. I'm getting a bit tired of smelling fishy all the time!"

Well—what an idea! No wonder Big-Ears' cat wouldn't leave Noddy for a single minute!

NODDY wears a little blue hat, and on the very end of it is a bell that tinkles. It makes quite a noise when he nods his head, and everyone knows Noddy is coming.

"Tinkle, tinkle! Here comes Noddy!" they say, and sure enough he trots round the corner.

Now once Noddy lost his bell. He was at Big-Ears' toadstool house, and Big-Ears was cooking dinner. He had made some sausage-rolls, and a cherry-pie.

Noddy liked watching Big-Ears when he cooked. Everything smelt so nice, and Big-Ears was a good cook.

"Can I put the cherries in the pie, Big-Ears? Oh, do let me," said Noddy. "I'll arrange them very carefully."

"You don't need to," said Big Ears. "Just empty them in. Oh, all right—if you *want* to spend half an hour putting them in one by one, I don't mind. You really are a baby, little Noddy!"

NODDY PUT THE CHERRIES IN THE PIE ONE BY ONE. HE
ARRANGED THEM ALL VERY CAREFULLY

It was after Big-Ears had finished his cooking that Noddy noticed his bell wasn't ringing. "Big-Ears," he said, "my bell has lost its ring."

Big-Ears looked to see the bell. "It's the *bell* that's lost!" he said. "I told you it was getting loose. Now you must hunt all over the house for it. It's somewhere in this room, that's certain."

But although Noddy and Big-Ears hunted in every single corner they couldn't find the bell. They looked under the table and in the coal-scuttle and in the sink and behind the book-shelf, but there wasn't any sign of the bell at all.

Noddy was very upset. "I don't feel myself without the bell jingling on my cap," he said. "I do miss it, Big-Ears."

"I miss it too," said Big-Ears. "But *what* can have happened to it? You certainly had the bell on your hat when you came in this morning—and you've been in this room all the time."

"Will a bell like that cost a lot of money?" asked Noddy. "I expect it will. It had such a nice little jingle. I haven't even a penny in my money-box, Big-Ears. Have you?"

"Yes, I've got a little money," said Big-Ears. "But not enough. Never mind, Noddy, come and eat your dinner. The sausage-rolls are ready, and the pie is just right. Cherry pie! You'll like that."

"I shan't," said Noddy gloomily. "I don't feel like dinner today, because I've lost my bell. I don't think I can eat anything."

He wouldn't eat even half a sausage-roll. Big-Ears was upset. He cut the cherry pie and put some on his own plate. Then he looked at Noddy.

"Have some pie," he said. "It's horrid to eat dinner all by myself. Have some, Noddy."

"All right," said Noddy, in a sad little voice. So Big-Ears put some on his plate too. Noddy took up his spoon and fork. He put some in his mouth—yes, it really was delicious.

And then he gave a shout, and made Big-Ears drop his spoon in surprise. "Big-Ears! BIG-EARS! I've found my bell!"

"Where? Where?" cried Big-Ears, looking all round the room.

"On my plate! In the cherry-pie!" said Noddy happily, and he fished the bell out from under a piece of crust with his spoon. "Look—here it is! Oh, Big-Ears, you baked it in the pie! Will it mind?"

"I don't know. See if it rings," said Big-Ears, quite excited.

Noddy shook it. Jingle-jingle-jingle! Yes, it rang beautifully.

"It must have dropped off your hat into the pie when you were putting in the cherries," said Big-Ears. "Oh, what a good thing we found it. Now, Noddy, do you know what you are going to do directly you've finished your dinner?"

"Yes," said Noddy. "I'm going to sew the bell on my hat again—very VERY tightly, Big-Ears!"

Noddy's Car

Parp-parp!
Get out of the way,
My car's in a terrible hurry today!
Run, you rabbit,
And jump, little dolly,
Please get out of my way, Miss Golly!
I'm taking this Teddy
To catch the bus,
He thinks we shall miss it, he's making a fuss!
Parp-parp!
Get out of the way,
My car's in a TERRIBLE hurry today!

NODDY GIVES A PICNIC

It was such lovely summery weather that Mrs. Tubby Bear thought it would be fun for Noddy to have a picnic. "Bruiny Bear can come," she said, "and ask little Tessie Bear. And Floppy Bunny can come and Connie Kitten."

So here goes Noddy in his car to ask them all. Floopy Bunny was pleased and thanked him very much.

Connie Kitten looked out of her big eyes at Noddy and was excited to think of such a fine picnic.

Tessie Bear said of course she would come and she would bring some gingerbread she had made.

And Bruiny Bear said he would bring his toy gun to frighten off the red goblins if they came.

Well, Noddy was very busy indeed, getting ready for the picnic. He went to the baker's. . . . And bought buns and biscuits and a great big cake. . . .

He went to the greengrocer's and bought tomatoes and plums and bananas—look at them!

And Mrs. Tubby Bear made egg, cucumber and tomato sandwiches in heaps.

Tricky Teddy, Gilbert Golly and Cheeky Rabbit were very cross because *they* hadn't been asked.

"Let's spoil their picnic," said Tricky. "I know where they're going—on the top of Breezy Hill."

"*I* know what we'll do," said Cheeky Rabbit. "We'll wait till they are just beginning their picnic. . . .

Then we'll call out 'Danger! Red goblin!' And they'll all rush away and *we'll* eat the picnic!"

Well, the day came for the picnic. Noddy took Tessie Bear and Connie Kitten in his car. . . .

And Bruiny Bear took Floppy Bunny at the back of his tricycle. Here they go up to Breezy Hill!

What fun it was to spread a cloth on the grass, and put out all the food—what a LOVELY lot! They all sat down to have their feast. Noddy passed Tessie Bear some sandwiches. "Do have one," he said.

And Bruiny Bear poured out the lemonade. There was plenty of everything, and they were all happy.

Suddenly there came a shout from behind a bush. "Red goblins! Run, run! The red goblins are coming!"

Oh dear, what a to-do there was then! Noddy hurried Tessie and Connie to his car, and drove off. . . .

And Bruiny Bear went off on his tricycle with Floppy Rabbit. All the lovely picnic was left behind!

And then Tricky, Gilbert and Cheeky crept out of their hiding places, laughing loudly. "Ho ho ho!"

"Now for a picnic!" said Tricky. And he handed out the sandwiches and poured some more lemonade.

Now on his way home, Noddy met Big-Ears on his bicycle, and stopped to tell him what had happened.

"*I'll* go and see those red goblins!" said Big-Ears in a rage, and off he went . . . *how* surprised he was . . .

When he peeped round a bush to see Tricky, Cheeky and Gilbert gobbling up the food.

Big-Ears went off to some red goblins he knew. "I want you to give someone a fright," he said.

Well, goblins like doing that—and my goodness me, what a shock those bad toys had! The goblins burst on them, shouting and howling, and what a time they gave Tricky, Cheeky and Gilbert!

The three bad toys rushed down a rabbit-hole to hide, and Big-Ears sent a squirrel to Noddy . . .

"Tell him to bring everyone back," said Big-Ears. So here come Noddy and the others again . . .

All were most surprised to find their picnic still there. "The red goblins *did* come," said Big-Ears . . .

"But only to frighten away those bad toys. Shall we give a bun each to the goblins, Noddy?"

So they did—but they didn't give anything at all to Tricky, Cheeky and Gilbert, howling down the rabbit hole.

"Thank you, Big-Ears!" said Noddy. And what a lovely time they had . . . just see how empty the dishes are!

CAN YOU FIND THE TWINS?

Noddy and Big-Ears meet some nice little elves. One pair of them wear the same
clothes and are twins. Can you find the twins?

24

NODDY WORKS HARD

One morning Noddy was on his way to Big-Ears' toadstool house in the middle of the wood. Parp-parp! That was Noddy hooting at Robbie Rabbit who *will* play ball in the middle of the road!

Ah—here is Big-Ears' house. Are you at home, Big-Ears? Rat-a-tatta-tat! Noddy knocks loudly.

"Come in!" called Big-Ears. "You've just come in time, Noddy—I'm going away for a few days."

Noddy was most surprised to find Big-Ears so busy packing his bag. "Why—where are you going?" he asked.

"My brother, Little-Ears, isn't well," said Big-Ears. "Now I must get my bicycle!" He hurried out. . . .

And will you believe it, his bicycle was gone! "Stolen!" said Big-Ears. "Oh—how *am* I to get to Little-Ears?"

"Take my car, Big-Ears," said Noddy, at once. "Go on—I'll find lots of jobs to do without my car."

"Thank you, Noddy!" said Big-Ears, and he drove off at once, and Noddy waved to him as he went.

Well, Noddy had to find some work to do, now that his car was gone. So he asked Mrs. Tubby Bear for some.

"You can hang up all my washing on the line," she said. "It's in the basket. Peg it up nicely."

So he began to peg it up—but Mrs. Tubby's biggest tablecloth fell down on him, and . . .

What a long time it took him to crawl out from underneath it! Mrs. Tubby Bear laughed and laughed!

Then Mr. Monkey asked him to come and water his garden flowers, so here he is watering a climbing rose. . . .

And when Miss Puss Cat passed by, he saw her flowery hat over the wall and watered that too, quite by mistake!

She wasn't at all pleased—but oh, how Mr. Monkey laughed. "It's worth sixpence to have a laugh like that!" he said.

After that little Noddy went to sweep Mr. Big Golly's chimney, and got himself as black as a golly. . . .

And Mrs. Big-Golly thought he *was* a golly, and tried to put him to bed with all her little gollies!

"I don't think I like not being a taxi-driver," said Noddy. "I don't do other jobs very well." He counted out his money. "I'll soon have enough to buy Big-Ears a new bicycle," he thought.

"Then I can have back my car." He went to do some gardening for Mr. Jumbo, but Jumbo's spade was so very big. . . .

And so was his watering-can that Noddy *had* to give up that job. So he went to the Noah's Ark . . .

And asked Mr. Noah for a job. "You can count all the animals for me, and see if there are two of each," said Mr. Noah.

But the animals were very naughty and simply *wouldn't* keep still for Noddy to count!

And Mr. Noah said that Noddy was quite wrong when he told him there were at least six of every animal!

Noddy was getting very tired of having odd jobs, but he didn't give up. He went to a red goblin . . .

And asked for a job with him, because goblins paid very well indeed. "Now let me see . . . you can clean the bicycle out in my shed," said the goblin. So Noddy went to get the bicycle. . . .

And will you believe it—it was Big-Ear's very own bicycle! The goblin had stolen it and hidden it. . . .

So, of course, Noddy jumped on it and rode straight away to Mr. Plod, and told him the news.

"I'll be after that goblin at once!" said Mr. Plod. "Big-Ears is coming back today. . . .

"He *will* be pleased." Well, Noddy rode Big-Ears' bicycle to Toadstool House—and hip hurrah. . . .

Big-Ears arrived at that very moment in Noddy's car. Parp-parp! How pleased they all were!

"Dear Big-Ears—I found your bicycle!" said Noddy. "And oh, I made a lot of money to buy you a new one. . . .

"So now I feel quite rich. I'll get into my car with you, and drive away to my little house. . . .

"And we'll have a lovely feast!" So here they are, very happy to be together again!

OH NODDY, NODDY!

BIG-EARS came along on his bicycle and knocked loudly on Noddy's door. Bang-bang-bang. Was Noddy in?

Nobody called "Come in!" Nobody came rushing to the door.

"Noddy must be out," said Big-Ears to himself. "But yet his car is outside. Perhaps he's asleep. I'll look in at the window and see."

He peeped in at the window—and dear me, Noddy was at home after all. He was sitting on a chair, with tears pouring down his cheeks, his head nodding very sadly indeed.

Big-Ears rushed to the door and opened it. He ran in and put his arms round Noddy.

"What's the matter, Noddy? What's happened?" Big-Ears said to him. "Have you hurt yourself?"

"Oooble, ooble-ooble," said Noddy, trying to talk with his mouth closed.

"What's that you're saying?" asked Big-Ears, astonished. "Open your mouth and talk properly, Noddy."

"OOOBLE-OOOBLE-OOO!" said Noddy, still with his mouth closed.

"I can't understand a word!" said Big-Ears. "Whatever has happened to you? Has someone put a spell on your mouth so that you can't talk properly?"

"OOO-OO-OOOBLE," said Noddy, as loudly as he could. He waved something at Big-Ears, and the brownie looked to see what it was.

"A tooth-brush!" he said. "Have you been cleaning your teeth, Noddy?"

Noddy nodded his head up and down without stopping.

"Well," said Big-Ears, puzzled, "cleaning your teeth doesn't make you act like this! Where's your toothpaste?"

Noddy pointed to a shelf and Big-Ears went to get the little tube of paste there. But there were two tubes—

one was marked "Best Tooth-paste for Toys" and the other one was not tooth-paste at all!

Big-Ears looked at it, and then he looked again. Then

he began to laugh and laugh.

"Oh my goodness me, Noddy!" he said. "Whatever *will* you do next? This isn't tooth-paste why, It's GLUE!"

Noddy nodded his head sadly, and pointed to his mouth. "Ooooble-ooble-ooo," he said, keeping it tightly shut because he couldn't possibly open it.

"Didn't you taste a fishy taste when you used it, you little silly?" asked Big-Ears. "Glue always tastes of fish!"

Noddy's head nodded again, and more tears trickled

down his cheeks.

"Now listen," said Big-Ears. "We've got to get your mouth open somehow so that I can wash out the glue. So I think I'd better make you sneeze—then your mouth will fly open—and you must *keep* it open—see?"

Noddy nodded up and down quickly. What a good idea! He stopped crying at once. Big-Ears went to the cupboard and took out Noddy's pepper-pot.

He held it under Noddy's nose. "Now sniff!" he said. "Not very hard, Noddy—just a *little* sniff!"

But Noddy sniffed very hard indeed, and a most ENORMOUS sneeze came! A-WHOOOOOOOSHOO-OOO!

It blew Noddy's mouth wide open. It blew him off his chair—and it made Big-Ears jump so much that he dropped the pepper-pot. Pepper flew everywhere, and Big-Ears began to sneeze too.

"WHOOOOOOSH! A—WHOOOOSH! Don't you shut your mouth now, Noddy. Keep it open, keep it open—oh, I'm going to sneeze again—WHOOOOOOSH!"

Well, it took quite a long time to clean the glue from Noddy's teeth, because they both kept sneezing—but at last it was done. Big-Ears looked anxiously at each tooth. Yes—they were all white and clean now.

"Can you talk, Noddy?" he asked. "Try."

"Yes, I can, Big-Ears—Oh, yes, I can talk properly again!" cried Noddy. "I can sing, too—listen!

"Oh what a silly thing to do
To clean my lovely teeth with glue!
It had a horrid fishy taste
And was a really dreadful waste.
I couldn't laugh, I couldn't speak,
And tears went rolling down my cheek.
Oh WHAT a silly thing to do,
To clean my lovely teeth with glue!"

Big-Ears laughed. "Ho, ho ho—how did you think of *that* song, Noddy! Now—you won't mix up those tubes again, will you? I don't want to hear you've cleaned your teeth with a tube of shoe-cream!"

That made Noddy laugh—and in the middle of his laugh he wanted to sneeze again.

"A-Whoooooosh-oo! Oh dear, you're sneezing too, Big-Ears! We shall go on doing this all day!"

So they will. It makes me want to sneeze too—a-a-a-a-WHOOOOOOSH-oo!

NODDY AND THE APPLES

ONE hot afternoon little Noddy went to the farm to ask for some eggs. "You must wait a while," said the farmer's wife. "I haven't been to collect the eggs the hens have laid yet."

"I'll wait then," said Noddy. "I'd like a rest. I'm so hot."

"Well, there's a nice breeze coming up," said the farmer's wife. "Go and sit under a tree."

So off went Noddy and sat down under a tree. He leaned against it and shut his eyes. Soon he was fast asleep.

Now, he was under an apple tree and the apples were very ripe. When the breeze blew it loosened an apple, and down it fell, plop, on to Noddy's head, and then rolled away.

Noddy woke up with a jump. He saw the apple rolling away. He looked all round, very cross.

"Who's throwing apples at me? Was it you, hen? Or you, pig? Let me tell you this—you'll be sorry if you throw things at *me*! I can throw things too, you know."

"Cluck," said the hen, in surprise.

"Grunt," said the pig.

Noddy shut his eyes again, and was almost asleep when another apple fell, plop! It bumped on to his nose this time and he sprang up in quite a rage.

"Was that you, goat? I can see you standing there! Or was it you again, pig?"

"Bleat," said the goat, and turned his back on Noddy.

"Grunt," said the pig. "Grunt!"

Noddy sat down again—and for a third time an apple fell—right on to his middle and took all his breath away. And then Noddy went mad.

He picked up the apples and threw them at the pig. He picked up some turnips and threw them at the goat. He shouted at the hens who came to see what was the matter.

The farmer came up to see what was going on. Noddy didn't see him, and flung a smelly old turnip at the goat. It missed him and hit the surprised farmer.

"Now!" he said. "NOW! What's all this? How dare you throw things at my animals, Noddy!"

"Well, they started it," panted Noddy. "Every time I sat down under this tree they threw apples at me. Feel this bump on my head!"

Plop! Another apple fell from the tree and hit Noddy on the shoulder. He looked up into the branches in surprise. "It must be someone up in the tree," he said.

"It's the wind in the tree," said the farmer, beginning to smile. "It's blowing the apples down. Oh, Noddy—what silly things you do! Now just say you're sorry to the goat and the pig and the hens."

"I'm sorry, I'm sorry, I'm sorry," said Noddy, going very red, and he ran to his car, got into it and drove away as fast as he could. Oh dear—what a good thing the farmer didn't spank him!

Hey, Noddy, come back. COME BACK! You've forgotten to take your eggs, you little silly!

HOW NICE IT IS TO GO AWAY

"How nice it is to go away
  And have a lovely holiday;
  And yet although it's fun to roam,
  It's even better coming home,
  Coming home—
  Coming home—
  It's really LOVELY coming home!"

TOY TOWN

NODDY
AND THE MAGIC BOOTS

One afternoon, when Noddy was out walking by himself because it was such a lovely day, he went into Be-Careful Wood. Its name was a very good one . . .

Because you just had to be careful in that wood. All kinds of queer people lived there. There was Pop-Out, who lived in a big oak tree with a door. Do you see it?

When Noddy went by, Pop-Out behaved like his name. He popped out of his tree with a yell and gave Noddy such a fright that he fell over—bump!

Another queer person who lived in Be-Careful Wood was Mr. Stumps. He could make himself look just like the stump of an old tree . . .

And when Noddy sat down on the strange little stump Mr. Stumps began to crawl away with Noddy. Oh dear, what a shock Noddy got! He got up and ran away quickly.

"No wonder Big-Ears has warned me not to walk here," he said. "But I'm really quite old enough now. Hallo—who's this coming along, smiling all over his face?"

An old pedlar came along, carrying a big tray of goods in front of him. "Hullo," he said to Noddy. "I'm Mr. Grin. Can I sell you anything today? What about this hat?"

"No, thank you," said Noddy. "I like my own hat. It's got a bell." "Well," said Mr. Grin, "what about a nice pair of shoes? Yours are really very babyish, you know."

"Dear me, are they?" said Noddy. "Well, perhaps I will try on a pair of shoes. These bright-green ones look nice." So he sat down to try them on—yes, they fitted well!

"Stand up and walk about in the shoes," said Mr. Grin, smiling in a most friendly fashion. "They're very cheap. They certainly suit you. Are they comfortable?"

Noddy was walking about proudly. "Yes—they're lovely," he said. "Walk to that tree and back," said Mr. Grin. So Noddy set off to the tree—but what's this . . .

He couldn't walk back! He had to go walking on—and on and on. He couldn't stop! "Hey, there's a magic spell in these shoes!" shouted Noddy. "Tell them to walk back!"

Mr. Grin laughed and laughed. "Those shoes will take you to my master, Mr. Frown-Hard," he called. "I often get servants for him by this little trick. Goodbye!"

Well, Noddy could hardly believe his ears! To think that Mr. Grin had got him to try on a pair of shoes that had a walk-away spell in them—and now he was off to Mr. Frown-Hard!

Poor Noddy! Look at him walking on and on, down this winding path and that, through the trees, all by himself. He can't stop. The shoes won't let him!

Noddy walked on till night-time came and the moon came out. At last he walked right out of Be-Careful Wood and came to a small hill. On the top was a cottage.

It had eight chimneys, and four doors in a row in the front. How queer! Was this where Mr. Frown-Hard lived? Yes—there he is, peeping out of the window, waiting for a new servant.

All the four doors flew open at once, and the shoes took Noddy to one of them. In he went. The doors shut. Oh dear! Now how will anyone ever know where Little Noddy is?

Noddy's little car was lonely in its garage without Noddy. Where was he? Why didn't he come and drive it? Ah, here was somebody opening the garage doors . . .

But it wasn't Noddy. It was Big-Ears. Big-Ears had come to see why Noddy hadn't visited him. He was astonished to find that Noddy's house was empty.

And here he was, peeping in the garage to see if Noddy had gone away in his car. How surprised he was to see the car there, all by itself, looking very sad.

"Something has happened to Noddy!" said Big-Ears. "Come along, little car. We'll go and look for him." So he got into the car and drove off. Parp-Parp!

"Noddy always wanted to go to Be-Careful Wood, so maybe he went there," thought Big-Ears—and here he is, driving carefully through the wood.

Very soon they met a pedlar. It was Mr. Grin, with his tray of goods in front of him. "Buy, buy, buy!" he cried. And then Big-Ears saw something on the tray that made him stare!

45

What did Big-Ears see on Mr. Grin's tray? He saw Noddy's shoes, red with blue laces. In a trice he was out of the car and had got hold of Mr. Grin.

He shook him hard. "Where did you get those shoes? Tell me before I turn you into a stone and throw you in the stream! Quick, tell me!"

Mr. Grin forgot to smile. He went down on his knees and begged for mercy. "Don't put a spell on me. I'll tell you where I got them from, I will, I will."

Soon Big-Ears knew how Noddy had put on the magic shoes and had had to go on walking till he came to Mr. Frown-Hard's house. How he glared at Mr. Grin!

"Have you another pair of shoes with the same kind of spell in them? You have? Well, put them on—and lead us to Mr. Frown-Hard's cottage. Quick!"

And now here is poor Mr. Grin, wearing magic shoes, plodding through the wood on his way to Mr. Frown-Hard's house. And after him goes Big-Ears in the car.

Now Mr. Big-Ears and Mr. Grin had come to Mr. Frown-Hard's cottage with its eight chimneys and four doors. Big-Ears knocks at every one of them in turn—blam-blam-blam-blam!

They all fly open at once! Big-Ears goes in at one, Mr. Grin goes in at another, and the little car drives itself in at a third—parp—parp—parp!

Out of the fourth door rushes Mr. Frown-Hard in alarm. Look who is chasing him with a big broom—Little Noddy! Oh, how pleased he is to see dear old Big-Ears!

"We'll lock Mr. Grin in the house," said Big-Ears with a smile as broad as Mr. Grin's was. Slam, slam, slam, slam—all four doors were shut and locked.

And away drove Big-Ears and Noddy, with Mr. Grin peeping dolefully through a window. "He should be called Mr. Sulk now," said Noddy. "Oh, it is nice to be in my car again!"

Well, you can guess what a tea-party they had that day when they all got back to Big-Ears' house. Even the little car was allowed indoors. Parp-parp! What a treat!

THE LITTLE PINK RABBITS

NODDY had five dear little passengers one afternoon. They were all small pink rabbits with ribbons round their necks.

They were going to have a picnic on Bluebell Hill, and they had a basket of food with them. What fun they were going to have!

Noddy set them down on the hill. "I'll come and fetch you at half-past five," he said. "Have a nice time!"

At a quarter past five he set off in his car to fetch them. On his way he passed a small golly, sitting at the side of the road, with a basket beside him. He was just stuffing a big bun into his mouth when Noddy passed.

"Somebody else having a picnic," thought Noddy. "I'll ask Big-Ears if he'll have one with *me* tomorrow."

Now, before he reached Bluebell Hill what did he see but all the five pink rabbits hiding under a hedge, looking as scared as could be. He stopped his car at once, and they came running over to him.

"Oh, Noddy, Noddy! We're so glad you've come! Have you seen the fox?"

"What fox? No, of course not," said Noddy. "Why? What's happened?"

"Oh dear! We were just going to begin our picnic when a golly came running up, calling out 'Fox! Fox! He's looking for rabbits! Beware!' So we had to leave our picnic and run away!"

"You poor little things," said Noddy, very sorry for them. Then he suddenly remembered the golly he had seen picnicking by the road. Oh, the bad little thing! He must have called out "Fox!" just to frighten the rabbits, and then taken their picnic things!

Noddy looked very fierce. He would punish that mean golly. He packed the little rabbits into his car and drove them home.

"*I'm* having a picnic tomorrow," he said. "You can all come to it—and I'll ask Big-Ears, too. But listen to me—I'm asking the Noah's Ark fox as well!"

"No, no!" squealed the rabbits, frightened.

"Yes, I am," said Noddy. "He's quite a friend of mine. He won't hurt you, I promise. We'll all run away when he comes—and then you'll see something funny happen!"

Noddy left them at their home, and then he went to fetch Big-Ears. They went together to the Noah's Ark, and asked Mr. Noah if the fox could come to a picnic with them the next day.

The fox was surprised and very pleased. He wasn't often asked out for a picnic. Noddy whispered

quite a lot of things into his ear, and he showed his sharp teeth in a grin.

"Yes. Yes, I quite understand," he said. "If you will really let me come to the picnic I'll do exactly as you say."

So the next afternoon Noddy, Big-Ears and the five pink rabbits went to Bluebell Hill again, with a basket of goodies. They had hardly sat down to eat when there came a loud shout, and the little golly came running up.

"Fox! Fox, I say! He's looking for rabbits to eat! Run, all of you, run! He's very fierce!"

Everyone got up and ran, Noddy and Big-Ears too. They didn't run very far, though—only to the nearest bushes! They hid there and peeped.

The golly sat down on the hill and took up a bun. And then something pounced out at *him*. It was the Noah's Ark fox! Noddy called out loudly.

"Fox! Fox! A fox who likes gollies! You said the fox would come, Golly, and he has! Look out!"

The golly gave a squeal of fright. He ran for his life—but the fox ran faster, and caught him. Aha! What a fine punishment for the mean little golly!

"Take him to Mr. Plod, the policeman," said Big-Ears to the fox, coming out from his bush. "We told him you'd carry the golly to him to be punished. Leave him there, Fox, and come back and enjoy the picnic with us!"

So the fox carried the howling golly away, and then came back again. He had to sit beside Noddy and Big-Ears because the rabbits really didn't like him very much —but he didn't mind a bit. It was *such* a treat to be asked out to a picnic!

WHAT A JOKE!

"OH bother!" said Noddy, "here come Tricky Teddy and Gilbert Golly. I *do* hope they won't tease me today!"

Noddy had been to see Big-Ears in Toadstool Wood, and he was walking home through the trees. Tricky Teddy grinned all over his naughty face when he saw Noddy.

"Let's take his hat and throw it up into that big tree," said Tricky to Gilbert Golly. So they ran at poor Noddy and snatched off his blue hat. Jingle-jing went the bell as the two scamps threw it high up into the tree.

"You're *mean*!" said Noddy, fiercely. "You know that tree's too big for me to climb."

"If you talk to us rudely we'll throw your shoes up as well," said Gilbert. "Take them off!"

"What's all this going on?" said a voice, suddenly, and Mr. Monkey walked up. "Oho—I see you've thrown Noddy's hat up into the tree—and you were just going to throw up his shoes too, weren't you?"

"It was just a joke, that's all," said Tricky Teddy. "Can't we play a joke?"

"Oh *yes*!" said Monkey. "*Any*one can play a joke. Jokes are fine. That blue hat looks funny up in the tree, doesn't it? It really makes me laugh—ha ha ha!"

Monkey suddenly snatched at Tricky's hat and threw it up into the tree too! "Another joke!" he said. "Oh, I do like jokes! Here, Gilbert, let me have your hat too."

And up into the tree went Gilbert Golly's hat as well. You should have heard Monkey laugh—he roared, and slapped Gilbert on the back. "Laugh!" he said. "It's a funny joke!"

Noddy couldn't help laughing too, because Tricky Teddy and Gilbert Golly looked so very, very surprised. But Monkey hadn't finished with them yet. Oh no!

He pulled at Gilbert's coat and off it came—and away it went up into the tree too! Gilbert could hardly believe his eyes.

"Don't!" he said angrily. "This isn't a joke—it's just silly. Stop it, Monkey."

"Now don't you start talking rudely to me, or I'll throw your shoes up as well," said Monkey. "Here, Tricky—give me your scarf—I'll play a joke with that too."

"No," said Tricky Teddy and he tied his scarf up well. "And you climb up and get my hat, Monkey. It's my best one. I'll get into trouble if you don't get it fo me."

"But I tell you, it's only a *joke*!" said Monkey. "It was only a joke when you threw Noddy's hat up, wasn't it? I heard you say so!"

"Well—yes, that was a joke," said Tricky, frowning all over his furry face. "But . . ."

"Then why isn't *this* a joke!" said Golly and he snatched Tricky's hanky out of his pocket—and away that went too. "Ho, ho, ho—laugh, Tricky, do laugh!"

"Oh don't throw any more things up into the tree, please, Monkey!" said Noddy. "We'll never be able to get them down. I can't BEAR to see my nice little blue hat up there."

"I'll get it for you," said Monkey, and up he went, climbing easily, swinging his long tail as he went. He got the hat, and then, hanging upside down by his tail, he threw it to Noddy.

Then down he came again. "Aren't you going to get *our* things too?" asked Gilbert.

"Dear me, no," said Monkey. "Come on, little Noddy—let's leave these jokers to laugh at *my* little jokes! Goodbye, you two—dear me, what long faces you've got!"

And off he went with little Noddy. Good old Monkey—he came along just at the right moment!

NODDY'S GOOD TURN
A game for two or more players

Whilst out in his car one day Noddy came across a little pink rabbit which had lost its way from the Ark. Noddy gave the rabbit a ride back, but it took him *such* a long time to find the way. Can YOU get there more quickly?

Ask Mummy for a different colour counter or button for each player, an egg-cup and a dice.
You then take turns to throw, but you must get a six to start.

NODDY GOES FISHING

One fine afternoon Noddy bought himself a fishing-rod and went fishing. He thought he would fish in the little lake nearby. So here he is, fishing away. Ah—he has caught something. Pull it in, Noddy, pull it in!

Well, what a strange thing—he has caught a little stool! "Ha! I'll give it to Big-Ears for his house," said Noddy.

He began to fish again. Another bite! What is it this time? A big fish? No—dear me, it's a small table!

"I'll give that to Mrs. Tubby Bear," said Noddy, pleased. "I wonder who has been throwing all this furniture away!"

Well, he fished again—and this time he fished up a little bed, and what a funny thing, it had sheets and blankets on!

They were wet, of course, but Noddy thought he could soon dry them. "This bed will do for Miss Fluffy-Cat," he said.

Do see what he has fished up by the end of the morning! Almost enough things to furnish a little house!

Everyone was very pleased with the things, especially Miss Fluffy-Cat who gave Noddy a big kiss for the dear little bed.

Well, the next thing that happened was a knock at Noddy's door, and when he opened it he saw a very angry person.

It was a little water-pixie, called Miss Bubble. "I hear that you have been fishing up my furniture," she said. "I live under the water."

"B-b-b-but I didn't know that!" stammered Noddy, very surprised. "Oh dear, oh dear—I've given it all away!"

The little water-pixie sat down and cried. Noddy couldn't bear it. He put his arms round her. "I'll build you a nice house," he said.

"Will you?" said Miss Bubble. "I don't really like living under the water. I'd rather live on land—on the bank of the lake."

So Noddy rushed off to get a box of bricks to build Miss Bubble a new house. Here he comes, staggering back.

He began to build the house beside the lake. Noddy—you've made a mistake. You've brought a railway station set!

Well! Miss Bubble stared at the railway station and she said she couldn't possibly live there. So Noddy took it down . . .

. . . and packed it up and went back for another building set. Here he is, with a much smaller box.

Oh dear, look what he has built this time! A fruit shop! "But I don't want a shop, Noddy!" said Miss Bubble.

Big-Ears came along, and how he stared. "I'll help you to pack it up and choose the right set," he said. "You're *such* a silly-billy, Noddy!"

Now look what Noddy and Big-Ears are building—what a darling little cottage! Everyone comes to watch. "There's the front door in!" says Noddy. "And, dear me, where's the chimney? Help me up with it, Big-Ears."

And now the house is finished, and Miss Bubble goes inside. "It's LOVELY," she says. "But it's very empty."

Then up came Miss Fluffy-Cat with the bed and Mrs. Tubby with the table, and Big-Ears went to fetch the stool . . .

And Mr. Jumbo brought some flowers, but the front door was so small he got stuck halfway in! But at last he got in.

Mr. Big Golly came with a blue teapot, and Sally Skittle with some cups and saucers, and Miss Wobble with a saucepan . . .

Everybody brought something for Miss Bubble's new little house. She danced all round, she was so happy.

"Oh! Oh! I've always wanted to live on land, it's so wet in the water!" she cried. "Noddy, do let's give a tea-party!"

Well, everyone likes a tea-party, of course, and off went Mrs. Tubby and Sally Skittle and the rest to get things to eat.

It was a dreadful squash inside the new little house, but nobody minded. All the little skittles sat on Jumbo's back . . .

And Mrs. Monkey let her children hang from the picture-rail by their tails.

"I shall call my house *Splash Cottage*," said Miss Bubble, cutting the big cake that Mrs. Tubby had brought.

"And I shall decorate it all round outside with shells. It will look beautiful. I really must give you a hug, Noddy, for being so nice."

Well, Miss Bubble did decorate her cottage outside with all kinds of shells. Doesn't it look lovely!

And will you believe it, *Splash Cottage* was so pretty that lots of people wanted to see it. And so, of course, Noddy was very busy . . .

. . . taking them to and fro in his little car. So it really was lucky for Miss Bubble and Noddy that he went fishing that fine afternoon!

NODDY
AND THE
FLYING ELEPHANT

One morning little Noddy got out his car as usual. He drove it out into the street to look for passengers. Now who would hail him first, and get in for a nice ride?

Be careful, Noddy—there is a big nail in the road! Can't you see it, sticking up a nasty sharp point? Oh dear, Noddy is heading straight for the nail—what a pity.

Bang! The nail goes into the tyre and the tyre bursts. Noddy puts on the brake and comes to a sudden stop. "I'm shot!" he says. "A gun went bang—and I'm sure I'm shot!"

Noddy wasn't shot, of course. He soon saw that his tyre had gone flat. He must pump it up quickly, or he wouldn't get any passengers that day. Now—where is the pump?

What a pity! Noddy left it behind that morning. Now what must be done? If he can't get his tyre blown up, his car won't go. Ah—here comes plump Mr. Panda. Perhaps he will help.

"I've got lots of breath," says Panda. "Perhaps I've got enough to blow up your tyre." So down he lies, and puffs air into the tyre—puff—puff—puff, pant—pant—pant!

But Panda hadn't got enough breath to blow up the tyre. Mr. Tubby Bear came up and thought he would try too. So here he is, trying his hardest to blow his breath into the tyre.

But no—he hasn't enough either. Noddy is very sad. Then Panda gives a shout. "Here comes Mr. Jumbo, the elephant. He has a fine long trunk. It's like a rubber pump, Noddy!"

So Noddy asked Jumbo to see if he could blow up his tyre with his long trunk. "Of course," said Jumbo, and he set his trunk to the valve of the tyre and puffed.

My goodness! Mr. Jumbo had so much puff that the rubber tyre swelled up at once! Look at it—it's getting bigger and bigger—and BIGGER! The car is tilting up!

"Hey!" cried Noddy. "The tyre is too big now. Much too big! Stop, Jumbo, stop puffing! You'll have to take some air out. Just look at the car, tilting to one side!"

Well, Jumbo stopped puffing—but, oh dear, the air rushed back up his trunk out of the tyre—and now look what is happening! Jumbo is swelling up instead of the tyre!

Poor Jumbo! He couldn't stop the air from the tyre making him swell and swell—and now he's so fat he's like an elephant balloon. He's standing up now, swaying about, and feeling queer.

The wind comes—and Jumbo is blown off his feet, because he is so full of air. "Noddy, catch me!" he cries. "I shall blow right up into the sky! Oh, oh, catch me, Noddy!"

But Noddy is too late to catch poor Jumbo—and off he goes up into the sky. Up and up and up. "Come back, Jumbo!" wails Noddy. "I don't like you being a big balloon!"

"*Ting—a—ling—a—ling*!" That's a bicycle bell—and who is this on the bicycle? Big-Ears, of course! Noddy rushes to him, and so do Panda and Mr. Tubby Bear. "Big-Ears, listen!"

Big-Ears is most astonished to see Mr. Jumbo floating in the sky like a big balloon. He stares and he stares, while Noddy tells him the story. "Good gracious!" says Big-

Ears. "We must follow Jumbo and see what happens to him. If the air goes out of him he will fall. Get on my bicycle, Noddy." So he and Noddy race away to follow poor Jumbo.

Jumbo didn't have at all a good time. It was such a windy day that he was tossed here and there, and once he even floated upside down. All his money fell out!

Then he bumped into something. It was a big kite with a face painted on it. "Now then, now then, look where you are going," said the kite crossly. "Bumping into me like that!"

Jumbo would have held on to the kite, but its face was so cross that he daren't. He floated on again—and good gracious me, what's that noise? *R—r—r—r—r—r—r!*

R—r—r—r—r—r! Why, it's a toy aeroplane in the sky making all that noise! Jumbo tried to get out of the way. The aeroplane circled all round him, and the pilot shouted:

"Hey there! What's the idea of floating about like this? You're dangerous! I shall report you. I nearly flew into you! *R—r—r—r—r!*" And away he flew to the west.

"I'm having a lot of adventures," thought Jumbo, "but I don't like them a bit. Ah—here's a nice cloud. I'll land on that and have a nice little rest!"

Jumbo sank down on the cloud. It gave a little beneath him, and he felt as if he was on a big soft cushion. He peeped down to the earth below. What a long way off it seemed!

But it was a pity he did that because his bicycle went straight into a ditch and upset them both. "I wish you had seen those stinging-nettles before you did that," said Noddy crossly.

Poor Jumbo fell through the hole he had made and found himself floating in the air once more. The wind came and had a fine game with him, blowing him this way and that!

Far below were little Noddy and Big-Ears, still pedalling madly to keep up with poor Jumbo. "Look, look, he's on a cloud now!" shouted Noddy; and Big-Ears at once looked up.

Jumbo saw them both far down below. "I'll shout to them and tell them to get a rope and lasso me," he thought. So he stood up on the cloud—but, oh dear, his foot went right through!

But now Noddy has a very good idea. He has seen a toy swan on a pond. "Look!" he says to Big-Ears, "let's ask that swan to rescue Jumbo. Swans can fly, can't they?"

"Hey, swan! Come here!" shouted Big-Ears; and the big swan came. Noddy pointed out Jumbo in the sky. "Can you go and rescue him?" he asked. "Please do, swan, he's so unhappy!"

So the swan flew up into the air at top speed, its great wings making quite a gale as it flew. It's getting close to Jumbo, closer and closer—and closer. Hey Jumbo, look round!

At last Jumbo sees the swan, and when it gets near to him he clutches it round the neck. "Dear good kind swan!" he says. "Oh, how glad I am to see you. Fly down with me, do!"

The swan flew down with poor Jumbo. When they got to earth, Jumbo fell off with such a bump that all his breath flew out of him, and he wasn't enormous any more!

He could walk properly. He could stand up in the wind! Oh, how glad he was. And now look—what's this? Why, it's Noddy's car, driven by Mr. Tubby Bear. The tyre is mended. How grand!

And home they all go, very happy again, Mr. Tubby and Big-Ears on the bicycle, and Noddy and Mr. Jumbo in the car. "I'll never blow up a tyre again," says Jumbo. "Never!" And I don't expect he will!

69

HE BARKS AND HE JUMPS

"He barks and he jumps,
His tail wags and thumps,
He leaps in the air like a frog!
He yelps and he runs,
He gobbles up buns,
This bumpity,
    thumpity,
        jumpity,
            terrible
                DOG!"

70

STOP, NODDY, STOP!

ONE afternoon Noddy took his car to have something mended in its insides. Big-Ears said he could borrow his bicycle for the rest of the day, if he liked.

So Noddy rode off on Big-Ears' little bicycle, feeling very pleased, because Big-Ears hardly ever let him ride it.

"I'll buy Big-Ears a big ice-cream for lending me his bicycle," thought Noddy. So he went to the ice-cream shop. He stood his bicycle by the kerb and went in to buy the ice-cream.

He came out with a beauty. It was a vanilla ice in a cone, with two red cherries on top. How pleased Big-Ears would be!

Holding the ice-cream carefully, Noddy went to the kerb. He got on the bicycle and rode off, holding the handle with one hand. Dear me, it was difficult to keep one eye on the ice-cream and the other on the road!

Then he heard a shout behind him. "Hey there! Stop! Stop, Noddy, stop!"

Noddy looked round and almost dropped the ice-cream. He saw a small elephant chasing him, waving his trunk to and fro as he shouted. "Stop, I say!"

Noddy didn't know the elephant. He pedalled faster still.

"He wants to snatch my ice-cream," he thought. "Elephants like ice-cream. He wants mine! Well, I'm NOT going to stop. He can shout his head off."

The elephant panted along behind on all four feet. "Stop, Noddy, stop! That's mine. STOP!"

"Well I never!" said Noddy to himself crossly. "So he thinks my ice-cream is his, does he? Just like an elephant. I've paid for it, haven't I?"

He pedalled on to Big-Ears' house. The elephant still lumbered behind, shouting angrily, but at last Noddy left him far behind. Good!

Noddy got off the bicycle at Big-Ears' little front gate. He wheeled it up the front path to the door. Then he called to Big-Ears.

"Big-Ears! Oh, there you are. Look, I've brought you an ice-cream. It's melting a bit, so you'll have to eat it quickly."

"Have a bit of it," said Big-Ears, holding it out to Noddy.

"No thank you," said Noddy. "I'm just going to lick the ice-cream drips off my tie. There's quite a lot there. Oh, Big-Ears, I must tell you about the elephant who shouted at me."

"Why did he shout?" asked Big-Ears, licking the big ice-cream.

"I think he wanted your ice-cream. He kept saying it was his," said Noddy. "Oh my—look, here he comes up the path! And shouting all the time, too!"

"Hey there! How dare you go off like that," cried the elephant. He came right up the front path and then took hold of the bicycle. Noddy leapt at him.

"Don't you dare to take Big-Ears' bicycle! You bad elephant!"

The elephant glared at him. "Are you mad? This is *my* bicycle!" "It certainly isn't *mine*," said Big-Ears, looking at it. "Oh, Noddy—what have you done with *my* bicycle? You've come home on somebody else's."

"Yes. On *mine*!" said the little elephant angrily. "And he wouldn't stop when I shouted, either!"

Noddy wailed loudly. "Oh dear! I'm sorry, I'm sorry, I'm sorry! But where is Big-Ears' bicycle then?"

THE ELEPHANT CAME RIGHT UP THE FRONT
PATH AND TOOK HOLD OF THE BICYCLE.

"Outside the ice-cream shop, where you left it, silly," said the elephant, mounting his bicycle and wobbling down the front path. "My bicycle was there, too—and you took mine instead of Big-Ears'."

"Oh dear!" wept Noddy. "I CAN'T go all the way back to the ice-cream shop. It's such a long way to walk. Stop, elephant, stop! Take me on the back of your bicycle. Stop!"

"Shan't," said the elephant rudely. "You didn't stop when I shouted at *you*—so *I* shan't stop either. *Good* afternoon!"

And off he went. Now poor Noddy has got to walk all the way back to Toyland Village to fetch Big-Ears' bicycle. I do hope it is still there!

15 16 17 18 19 20 21 22 23
14 13 12 11 10 9 8 7 6 5 4 3 2 1

NO LICENCE BACK TO START

WHEEL LOS... BACK TO 1...

ANIMALS CROSSING MISS 2 TURNS

SHELTERING FOR RAIN MISS TURN...

BRINGING TOY-CAT HOME FORWARD TO 10

FORBIDDEN FOR CARS, BACK TO 60

68 67 69 70 71 72

ACCIDENT, BACK TO GARAGE NO 60

NODDY'S EXCITING RIDE
A game for two or more players

Noddy went off for a quiet ride in his car one day when he started to have the most amazing adventures before he reached his House-for-One. Play this game and follow Noddy's adventures in his car.

Ask Mummy for a different coloured counter or button for each player and a dice in an egg-cup. You then take turns to throw, but you must get a six to start.

76

NODDY AND THE NAUGHTY TOYS

One day Noddy went out in his little car to find some passengers to take to the station. Here he goes, parp-parp, and the bell on his hat jingles loudly.

First he took Miss Plump Doll, and she took up so much room that he could hardly steer. "You should make your car bigger," said Miss Plump Doll.

Then he took a small tin soldier, who rattled about on the seat, and nearly fell out. "You should make your car smaller, I'm nearly falling out!" said the soldier.

Noddy was rather cross with passengers who found fault with his car. His next passenger was a toy dog, who seemed very nice, until suddenly . . .

He leapt right out of the car to chase poor Miss Fluffy Cat down the road and round the corner. "He never paid my fare!" said Noddy. "What behaviour!"

"I shan't take any more passengers this morning! I'll just take myself for a nice little drive!" So here goes Noddy all by himself, parp-parp, parp-parp!

Now, on his way back home again, Noddy came to the bottom of a steep, winding hill. When he got there, somebody called to him. "Hey! Help me, will you?"

It was a golly with a very old car. It just *wouldn't* go up the hill! "Can you tow me up?" he said. "I'd be very glad if you could."

So here is Noddy tying the tow-rope to the car behind. Then he gets back into his car, and the golly gets into his. "Right away!" he cries.

Up the hill crawls Noddy's car, dragging the golly's car behind it. But look—here are two naughty boy-dolls running after it . . .

They have a little toy-cart. They fasten it to the back of the golly's car, and get in. Aha! They have a free ride up the hill now!

And now here is a little horse on wheels. He thinks he will hold on to the back of the boy-dolls' cart, and be dragged up too. What an idea!

Dear me, here comes a doll with a pram! What is she doing? She has jumped into the pram with the baby, and is holding on to the toy horse's tail!

And she is getting a free ride too. Noddy's car has gone round the corner. He is wondering why it is puffing and panting so much . . .

He doesn't know what a lot of things it is pulling—the golly's car—the little toy-cart, the horse on wheels—the doll in the pram!

A teddy bear on a tricycle saw the long row of things going up the hill, and he cycled up to the pram. Ah—if he holds the handle, he can be dragged up too!

And here is a wooden engine with two trucks. Clip yourself on to the back of the tricycle, engine, and you'll get a nice lift too!

Up the winding hill went the long, long row of things. Noddy was feeling quite alarmed for his car. It went more and more slowly. He didn't know why!

When Noddy's car was almost at the top, it stopped. Noddy looked round at the golly—and then he saw all the row of things stretching down the hill!

He scrambled out of his car. "What's all this! How dare you! You've tired my poor car out. You must *all* pay me two pence each!"

Noddy asked the golly for two pence. "Well, *my* car pulled the boy-dolls' cart," said the golly. "Hey, you dolls, give me two pence for the lift!"

"Well, *we* pulled along the horse on wheels!" said the boy dolls. "Hey, Mr. Horse, give us two pence for the lift!" The toy horse gave a neigh.

"I pulled along this pram behind me," said the horse. "Now, you doll in the pram, give me two pence please, and just leave go my tail!"

"My pram pulled along the teddy bear on the tricycle," said the doll in the pram. "He was very heavy. Teddy, give me two pence please, for your lift."

"Well, what about the engine and two trucks behind *me*?" said the teddy bear, quite cross. "I pulled *them*, didn't I? Engine, give me two pence."

"I haven't got two pence," said the engine. "I've only got two trucks. You can have those if you like." Well, well, it looked as if Noddy wasn't getting any payment at all.

And will you believe it, he was so cross that he undid the tow-rope that tied his car to the golly's car—what a thing to do!

Everything began to go down the hill again! And now it looked as if the two trucks and the engine were pulling everything along, instead of Noddy.

But they all went down the hill much too quickly, and the engine and the trucks ran straight into the pond. Splash! Be careful, you'll be next, teddy bear!

But the bear fell off his tricycle, and sat howling in fright. He only *just* got out of the way of the pram in time. He rolled himself away quickly.

The mother doll swung her pram aside just before it ran into the pond. Goodness, what a narrow escape! Look out, here comes the horse on wheels now!

He ran beside the pond, and fell over upside down, with all his wheels going round and round and round. What a job he will have getting up again!

As for the two boy-dolls, they couldn't stop their cart going into the pond—but it floated like a little boat, so they were quite all right!

The golly's car was going so very, very fast down the hill that it leapt right over the pond and landed on the other side . . .
What a surprise he got! Mr. Plod came up

at that moment, looking quite alarmed. "Is this a down-the-hill race or what?" he said, sternly.

As for Noddy, he is driving away crossly in his little car. "To think I pulled them all up the hill, and they never paid me a penny!" he says. "WHAT behaviour!"

NODDY AND THE EGGS

"NODDY! Please will you go and fetch me one dozen eggs from the farm," said Big-Ears, when he called one morning at Noddy's little house. "My brother Little-Ears is coming to dinner, and bringing a friend."

"Oh yes, Big-Ears. Of course I'll get the eggs for you," said Noddy. "I'll run up to the farm in my little car."

"If I'm not in when you bring them to my Toadstool House, pop them into my larder, please," said Big-Ears, getting on his bicycle and riding off again. "Sorry I can't wait. Just going to get a new loaf of bread and some butter."

Noddy was so afraid that he might forget to fetch the eggs that he wrote out a little note and put it into the driving seat of his car. He finished cleaning the car, and then fetched a basket and got into the driving seat.

"Ah—there's my note, with EGGS written on it," he said. "I'll go straight to the farm before I forget. Big-Ears doesn't like it when I don't do what he asks me to."

Away he went in his little car. Parp-parp! It hooted at pretty Angela Golden-Hair. Parp-parp! It hooted at Bruiny Bear. Parp-parp! It even hooted at Mr. Plod!

"Ah—there goes little Noddy," said everyone. "We

always know when *he's* about!"

Noddy soon came to the farm. Mrs. Straw was very busy making lovely yellow pats of butter in her little dairy.

"Hello, little Noddy," she said. "What do you want?"

"Twelve nice new-laid eggs, please," said Noddy. "Oooh, can I taste that butter?"

"No, keep your fingers out of it," said Mrs. Straw. "See how dirty your hands are! Dear, dear—I don't believe you washed them this morning."

"I did," said Noddy. "But I got them dirty again cleaning the car. Where are the eggs, Mrs. Straw?"

"Well, there now—I've sent them all off to the market," said Mrs. Straw. "But you can go and look in the nests, Noddy—I expect the hens will have laid some more. You can take a dozen."

So Noddy took his basket, and went to look for eggs in the nests. He went into the hen-houses, but not one single egg was in any of the nests.

He met a hen and spoke to it. "Hen—do you know where there are any eggs?"

"Cluck-cluck!" said the hen and scuttled away.

Then Noddy saw a hen sitting in a little wooden coop, on a nice big nest. "Hallo, hen," he said. "Have you any eggs there?"

"Cluck-cluck!" said the hen proudly, and got off her nest to show him a beautiful batch of white eggs.

"Oh, they're lovely!" said Noddy, and counted them. "Yes—you've twelve eggs. Just what I want!" And he picked them up one by one and put them into his basket.

"Cluck-cluck!" said the hen, angrily, and gave him a sudden peck on his hand.

"Oooh, don't," said Noddy. "That's unkind. There—that's all the eggs. I'd better take some of this soft hay, too, in case they joggle about and break when they are in my car."

Soon he was back in his car again, the basket of eggs beside him. What nice big eggs! Big-Ears would be very, very pleased!

Noddy drove carefully back to the toadstool house. He stopped, got out, and took the basket of eggs. He went up to the door and called loudly.

"Big-Ears! Are you back yet? I've brought the eggs."

There was no answer, so Noddy opened the door and went inside. The cat was there, dozing by the fire. "Hallo, cat," said Noddy. "I've brought the eggs for Big-Ears. I'm going to put them into the larder."

He opened the larder door and carefully put the eggs one by one into a dish, with the soft hay under them. Then he shut the door and went out. The cat didn't even look at him.

Now not long after Noddy had gone, the cat pricked up its ears. It could hear a strange noise somewhere. Yes— from the larder! Whatever could it be? It got up and strolled over to the door. Then it grew very excited and began to miaow, and to scratch at the door.

It was still doing this when Big-Ears came in with Little-Ears, and his friend, Mr. Whiskers Rabbit.

"Goodness—what's the matter with your cat?" said Little-Ears to his brother. "Is your larder full of fish or something?"

"No. What's the matter, puss? Why are you so excited?" said Big-Ears, going to the larder-door. "Get away from my feet."

Big-Ears opened the larder-door—and then he stared in

amazement! The larder shelves were full of tiny yellow chicks! The cat nearly went mad, and Little-Ears only just caught hold of it in time, or it would have leapt on the shelves to catch the chicks.

"Look at that!" said Big-Ears, as the tiny chicks scrambled about over his pies and tarts and sausage rolls.

"Wherever did they come from? Oh dear—I suppose it is a silly joke of Noddy's. I asked him to bring me some eggs—and he brought me chicks instead. Really, he's very foolish sometimes!"

Big-Ears caught all the tiny chicks and put them into a box so that the cat could not get them. He felt very cross

with Noddy. What a thing to do! Well, he would certainly scold him about it when he came along that afternoon.

He set out a nice meal for Little-Ears and Mr. Whiskers Rabbit. "I'm very sorry there are no eggs," he said. "And I don't expect anyone wants to gobble up one of those dear little chicks! Really—what a surprising thing to find in my larder!"

Just before tea there came a rap at Big-Ears' door. It was Noddy, hoping to be asked to tea. But Big-Ears was not smiling when he opened the door.

"Noddy," he said, in a stern voice, "I'm not pleased with you. Why did you bring me twelve chicks instead of twelve new-laid eggs?"

"I didn't," said Noddy, in surprise. "I went to choose the eggs myself at Farmer Straw's. Mrs. Straw said I could take any I found in the nests."

"Well, dear me—*where*

did the chicks come from then?" said Big-Ears, astonished. "Look, Noddy—they're in this box—the dearest little fluffy things! Who could have brought them? And where are the *eggs* you said you brought?"

Then suddenly Little-Ears began to laugh. He laughed and laughed, and Big-Ears stared at him in surprise.

"Oh Big-Ears—haven't you guessed what has happened?" said Little-Ears, chuckling. "Silly little Noddy here went to take eggs from a hen who was hatching

some out! Not new-laid eggs at all! And he brought them here, and put the eggs into your dish, with that hay we saw. . . ."

"Good gracious—and they all hatched out in my larder!" cried Big-Ears. "No wonder my old cat was so excited when she heard them cheeping there! I suppose the eggshells are in that dish. Well—what a thing to happen!"

"Oh dear!" said Noddy, in alarm. "What *will* Mrs. Straw say? Will she be very cross with me? What shall I do?"

"Put that box into your car and take back all the chicks," said Big-Ears. "Really, Noddy—fancy taking the eggs from under a sitting hen! Wasn't she cross?"

"Yes—she pecked me, look," said Noddy. "Oh dear—

I'm always getting into trouble. The hen will be angry with me, and so will Mrs. Straw."

"Well, it's your own fault," said Big-Ears. "You knew chicks came out of eggs, didn't you? So do ducklings—and sometimes little snakes come out of *snake*-eggs!"

"Good *gracious*!" said Noddy. "I'll never have an egg for my breakfast again! I just *won't* have a snake gliding about my breakfast table!"

"Now you take these chicks back to Mrs. Straw and let her give them to the mother-hen," said Big-Ears, "And then come back here and have tea with us. Well, well, well—I simply *never* know what you're going to do next!"

Noddy really is funny, isn't he? I do hope the mother-hen won't peck him again!

NODDY AND MR. TUBBY VISIT BIG-EARS

A game for two or more players

Noddy and Mr. Tubby set off in Noddy's car to go and see Big-Ears at Toadstool House but they have many stops on the way and it takes them a very long time. Can YOU get there more quickly? Ask Mummy for a different colour counter or button for each player and a dice in an egg-cup. You then take turns to throw, but you must get a six to start.

OH WHAT SHALL I EAT AT THE PARTY?

"Oh what shall I eat at the party?
Oh WHAT shall I eat at the party?
I think I will start
With a little jam-tart,
And then I will take
A big slice of cake,
And a chocolate bun
But only just one,
And a jelly that shakes
And quivers and quakes,
And some lemonade too,
And a biscuit or two,
And . . . well, I am sure
I can't eat any more!
That's what I'll eat at the party,
Yes, that's what I'll eat at the party!"

NODDY AND THE BIG BALLOON

Noddy sailed off on a cloud, sitting happily in his little car. "It's such a fine day, I'm floating away!" he sang. And look, he's gone quite a long way already.

But, dear me, a very strong wind began to blow, and a whole lot of black clouds piled up round Noddy. "I don't much like them," says Noddy, in alarm. "They're too big!"

And now the clouds are so thick that they have almost hidden Noddy and his car. You can only just see the two back wheels. "It's dark; I must hoot," says Noddy.

Then a storm came. The thunder roared and the lightning came. There's a flash, look—it has lighted up Noddy and his car on the cloud. How the wind is blowing them along!

And now the rain has come. Look at it falling on Noddy. "Where's my umbrella?" he cries; and he puts it up. "This isn't a nice adventure at all. I don't like it."

But soon the storm is over and the sun shines out again. Noddy is alarmed when he looks at his cloud. It isn't nearly as big as it was, and it has changed its shape!

"Why, there soon won't be any of my cloud left!" he says. "Oh, my goodness, what's that?" A loud noise came near him, and something shot by at a terrific rate.

"Perhaps if I use my steering-wheel I can steer the cloud towards it." So here is Noddy sitting in his car, steering towards the tall tree. Be careful, Noddy!

So on went Noddy, looking for something else to steer towards. He was feeling worried now, because the cloud was getting so very small. The wind kept blowing bits off it.

"An aeroplane, I suppose," said Noddy. "Good gracious! What a wind it made. I nearly got blown off the cloud. What's that over there? It looks like the top of a very tall tree."

Just as Noddy got to the top of the tree, the wind blew hard and the cloud flew right over the top and missed it. Bother! It wasn't any good steering back against the wind.

Good gracious! Whatever is this just below him. Noddy peers out to see. It's a big balloon, with a basket below it full of passengers. "Hey there! Look out!" cries Noddy.

But the balloon is rising steadily, and it bumps against Noddy's cloud. It breaks it up. Noddy feels the car jolting . . . Oh dear, oh dear, is it going to fall down?

No, it isn't. It is resting nicely on the very round top of the big balloon. How queer! Nobody down in the balloon basket knows that Noddy is up on top. Well, well!

Noddy yells loudly. "Hie, Hey! I'm up here! Hie!" That makes all the balloon passengers very puzzled indeed. Look at them leaning out. Who is calling and shouting like that?

The passengers in the balloon can't see Noddy, of course, because he is on the very top of the balloon. Noddy shouts again. "Where are you going, balloon people?"

"We're going to land on Tall Mountain—on the very top," called back one of the passengers, almost falling out because he leaned out so far to see who was shouting.

Then Noddy saw that ropes ran round over the top of the balloon. He tied his car up safely with one—and then he began to climb down one of the ropes. "Here I come!" he cried.

Noddy climbed right down to the balloon basket. The passengers were so frightened when they saw his legs appearing that they all cowered down. Noddy couldn't see anyone!

There was a sailor doll and a little black doll—and with them were two more dolls, both with very pretty curly hair. Noddy shook hands politely.

So off went Noddy in the balloon—doesn't it look queer with the little car on top? And, will you believe it, whenever they came to a cloud the car hooted at it.

He jumped into the basket, and the balloon swayed dangerously. "Don't be afraid," he said, "I'm only little Noddy." So then everyone stood up and looked at him, still scared.

"I'm sorry to burst in on you like this," said Noddy. "May I travel with you to Tall Mountain?" "Of course," said the sailor doll, and showed him a map. "It isn't far."

"There's Tall Mountain—look, there it is!" cried the sailor doll suddenly. And, sure enough, there it was. Can you see it, sticking right up into the sky! How big it is!

"We've come to Tall Mountain because there aren't enough houses to live in where we come from," said the little black doll. "We're going to build our own." See, they are nearly there!

Bump! They have come down suddenly. The gas is going out of the balloon. Look at it getting smaller and smaller! Noddy hurries to untie his car. The sailor doll helps him.

Now there is no balloon left, only the basket. Noddy is beside it with his car, and all the dolls are admiring it. "What a lovely car!" says one little curly-haired doll.

The dolls aren't quite where they want to be. They want to build their house right at the very very top of the mountain. So Noddy offers to take them in his car.

He can only take two at a time, so first he takes the sailor and the little black doll, then the others. My goodness me, what a wonderful view from the top!

"Thank you!" says the sailor doll. "Won't you stay with us, Noddy, and build a house too?" But Noddy shakes his head. "No, I must get back home," he says. But, oh dear—something's gone wrong!

Noddy can't make his car go! There he is, at the very top of the tall mountain, and his car won't start to take him home again. The sailor cranks it up but it's no use.

"Noddy, you've run out of petrol!" says the sailor doll, at last. "Oh well, I'll go and get some," says Noddy. But, dear me, there is no petrol sold at the top of a high mountain.

"I know, I know! Get in, Noddy, and we'll push the car off!" says the little black doll. "It will run all the way down the mountain by itself!" So here they all are, pushing hard!

And down the high mountain goes the little car at top speed. It doesn't need any petrol, the hill is so steep. It just runs down all by itself. How marvellous!

Now the car is running down a steep slope into Toyland—Noddy is coming into his very own village! *Parp*, *parp*, here we are back again! Out of the way, Golly, out of the way, Teddy!

And, will you believe it, the car was able to run right into its own little garage, tired after so many adventures! Noddy's safe home again—and isn't he glad!

I'VE CLEANED MY TEETH

"I've cleaned my teeth
  And I've brushed my hair,
I've polished my shoes
And I've time to spare
To drink my milk
And to eat my bread,

And I've plenty of time
To nod my head.
Nid-niddy-nod,
Nid-niddy-nod!
Plenty of time
To nod my head!"

GOOD MORNING

"The sun is shining
Up in the sky,
The birds are singing,
And so am I!
The bees are buzzing
As loud as can be,

The flowers are nodding
Their heads, like me!
The wind is blowing
The clouds along,
And I am singing
My little song!"

NODDY AND THE AEROPLANE

Now one morning Noddy was driving his car through Toy Village, when he saw Mr. Plod the policeman staring into the sky. Sally Skittle was staring up too, and so was Mr. Tubby Bear. "Good gracious!" said Noddy. "It's an aeroplane—very low!"

So it was. It was a gay little plane, painted cream and blue, but it was going very, very slowly, and coming down low. . . .

"Look out!" cried Noddy. "You nearly hit that chimney! Oh, my goodness, Mr. Plod, jump—he's going to land on you, I'm sure!"

The aeroplane didn't land on Mr. Plod, but it frightened him so much that he fell right over, and his helmet went very, very crooked. . . .

"Hallo!" said the pilot, jumping out. "Did I scare you all? You did look funny, with all your faces staring up at me!"

Mr. Plod got up, looking very angry. "How *dare* you fly so low and come down in our High Street?" he shouted angrily. "I couldn't help it," said the pilot. "I ran out of petrol. Hey, Noddy—can you get me a large can, please, at the garage?"

"You come along with *me*," said Mr. Plod. "I tell you, aeroplanes are *not* allowed to land here!" The monkey gave Mr. Plod a push. . . .

"Oh do be quiet," he said. "Here's some money, Noddy." Mr. Plod was very angry at being pushed. He caught hold of the monkey.

"I arrest you!" he said. But the pilot wriggled away, frightened. How could he escape? Ah—what about that little car?

And will you believe it, he ran to Noddy's car, leapt in, and drove off at top speed, knocking Sally Skittle over!

Noddy had gone to get the petrol, and he was most surprised when he came back with it, to find his little car gone!

"What! That monkey pilot has taken it!" he cried. "Well, I'll go after him—in his aeroplane!" See, he fills the tank . . .

With petrol, and now in he climbs to fly away. Oh *do* be careful, Noddy—you aren't used to planes!

And now away he goes into the air! He leans out and waves to Mr. Plod and the others. Whatever will he do next?

At first Noddy wasn't very good at flying. You're going too fast, Noddy—you nearly bumped into that tower!

"Hey—you're flying upside down!" shouted Mr. Plod. "Noddy, you'll fall out! That's not the right way to fly!"

"Now he's all on one side—oh, look, Noddy's falling out!" cried Sally Skittle. "No—he's slid back into his seat again!"

And then whir-rr-rrr-rrr! Noddy was away at top speed, looking for the monkey who has taken his little car.

"Mr. Plod shouldn't have frightened him so," said Noddy. "Oh there he is, far away down below." Yes, so he is!

The monkey driving Noddy's car heard the aeroplane above him, and hooted. "Parp-parp. Come on down here!"

"No!" shouted Noddy. "You take my car back to Mr. Plod and say you're sorry to him. I'm not coming down yet!"

So the monkey turned Noddy's car round, and here he is driving back to Mr. Plod, looking upset. Mr. Plod scares him!

Noddy flies up into the sky again, and bumps into a little cloud. "I'll have a rest," he says, and ties his plane . . .

To one end of the cloud—and now the wind blows the cloud along, and the cloud takes the plane along with it!

"I'd better fly back now, little plane," says Noddy, after a time. "Goodness me—I hope you know how to land yourself because *I* don't!" Down flies Noddy—and see, everyone is looking up again. BE CAREFUL. Noddy—that's the pond . . .

Noddy *nearly* landed on the pond—see the ducks quacking in fright! One of the plane's wings made such a splash!

Now he tries again. Noddy, you've hit a tree. See, he's stuck up there on the top, almost falling out. But the wind blows . . .

And the plane is off again. "COME DOWN!" shouts Mr. Plod. Noddy swoops again—over goes a lamp-post!

"Sorry, sorry, sorry!" yells Noddy, and Mr. Plod shakes his fist at him. Up goes Noddy again, feeling a bit scared.

And down he goes once more. LOOK OUT, Mr. Plod! There, the plane has knocked off his helmet!

But this time Noddy really does land, and the plane bumps into fat Mr. Jumbo and comes to a stop. Up runs Mr. Plod . . .

And Noddy leaps out in fright, just as the monkey pilot drives up in his car. Out he jumps and gets into his plane and Noddy runs for his car. Parp-parp, he's off and away. Whir-rr-rr! So is the aeroplane! Good gracious—*what* an adventure!

NODDY AND NAUGHTY GOBBY

Did I ever tell you about the trick that Gobby, the little green goblin, played on Noddy one day? Gobby hadn't a car of his own and every time he saw Noddy driving by he sighed.

"I wish I had a car like that. I wish I had. I'd just like to borrow it for a day or two. I wonder if Noddy would let me." So next time he saw Noddy in his car he stopped him.

"Noddy! Hey, Noddy! I want to ask you something. Please lend me your car for a day or two. Please, please do!" Noddy shook his head. "Certainly NOT. I wouldn't dream of it!"

Well, Gobby the goblin thought and thought about the car. He would have to borrow it somehow. So one day when Noddy came driving by in his car he called to him again.

"Noddy! You are very strong! I've caught a fish in this pond and it's so big I can't pull it out. If you pull it out I'll share it with you for our dinner."

Noddy stopped and looked. Gobby held a fishing-line, and he was pulling and pulling at it. My, it must be a big fish! "I'll pull it out easily!" said Noddy, and he went to help.

"Give me the line," said Noddy. "I'll soon drag the fish in." So he began to pull on the line. How he pulled! He pulled and he tugged, but he just couldn't drag that fish in!

Another goblin came by, grinning. "I'll help," he said, and he gave a hand too. Then they pulled together—but no, that fish still didn't show even a nose. Pull again, Noddy!

When the goblin and Noddy pulled once more something rose up out of the pond. Goodness, whatever is it? Well, well—it's just a great lump of wood! The line is tied to it.

"It's a trick!" cried Noddy fiercely. "Gobby tied the string to a log of wood and pretended it was a fish. Why did he do that? I'll give him such a biff!"

But where was Gobby? He had gone, and was nowhere to be seen. And where was the little car? That had gone, too. Noddy stared in horror and ran round looking for it.

"You're in the trick, too!" he shouted at the second goblin. "Now you just tell me where Gobby has taken my car!" The goblin turned and ran. Noddy was left alone.

Noddy had to walk all the way to Mr. Plod the policeman's. Soon Mr. Plod was writing down everything in his big black notebook. He grinned at Noddy.

"You be careful before you go fishing again!" he said. "Now cheer up—I expect we'll soon get your car back for you." Noddy went off to tell Big-Ears. He felt very gloomy.

Big-Ears was most surprised to hear the story. "Jump on to the back of my bicycle," he said. "We'll go and look for that goblin—and I shall take a few hard smacks with me for him!"

Noddy went off on the back of Big-Ears' bicycle. "We'll go and ask Mrs. Gobby if she has any idea where her son has gone," said Big-Ears. "Hold on tight—the road is very bumpy."

It certainly was. Noddy fell off three times, and then held on very tightly indeed to Big-Ears. Big-Ears gave a yell and fell off, too. "You're choking me!" he cried. "Don't hold so tight!"

Here they are at Mrs. Gobby's little tumble-down house at last. She didn't know at all where Gobby was. "You tell him he's got a spanking waiting for him at home!" she said.

Noddy and Big-Ears went to Gobby's old Granpa, but he couldn't tell them about Gobby either. "The scamp!" he said. "Tell him I've got a big stick for him here!"

And then who should they see coming along the road but Mrs. Long-Ears Bunny and her son Woffle-Nose. Woffle was limping and his head was bandaged up. Big-Ears stopped at once.

"What's happened?" he asked. "Oh dear!" said Mrs. Long-Ears. "Noddy's car knocked poor Woffle down. It didn't even stop. It was on the road to Bouncing Ball Village."

"Poor Woffle!" said Noddy, patting the little bunny. "I'm so sorry you got hurt. I wasn't driving my car—it was Gobby. I would never have hurt a nice little bunny like you."

"Well, all I can say is that I have a big slipper ready to spank Gobby with when I see him next," said Mrs. Long-Ears. "You go after him and get your car back, Noddy." So here they go!

"Off to Bouncing Ball Village!" said Big-Ears. "Gobby has a friend there, a big red ball. That's where he'll be." At last there is a sign-post that says: "This is Bouncing Ball Village."

Noddy and Big-Ears rode through the village, dodging the bouncing balls. Noddy called out to a green one: "Hey—have you seen a little red and yellow car, with a goblin driving it?"

"No," said the ball, and bounced right over the bicycle, making Noddy's hat-bell jingle. It bounced back and hit the bell again. "Don't," said Noddy. "My hat doesn't like that."

The two rode on again—and Noddy gave a sudden yell that made Big-Ears almost fall off in alarm. "My car! Over there, by that funny house! Look, Big-Ears, look!"

Yes, it was Noddy's car, and there was no one in it! Noddy leapt off the back of Big-Ears' bicycle and ran to it. But a big ball bounced up and knocked him right over.

He got up, and another ball knocked him down, and then bounced on him! Noddy got up and jumped into his car just before a third ball came up to have a bit of fun!

He hooted loudly and the balls bounced away in alarm. Noddy started the car—and at that moment Gobby ran out of the queer little house. "Hey, that's my car!" he cried.

Noddy drove fast out of Bouncing Ball Village. Big-Ears followed on his bicycle, trying to dodge a whole family of balls that rolled about round him. What a place!

He went to Mr. Plod at the police-station. "I've got my car back," he said. "But look—one wing is scratched and the bonnet is dented. Please catch Gobby as soon as you can."

Well, Gobby had to walk all the way back home on his two feet. It was a long, long way, and he got very tired of the balls rolling round his legs and bouncing on his head.

Mr. Plod caught the goblin the very next day. "I must put you into prison for taking Noddy's car," he said. "I only borrowed it for a day or two," said Gobby sulkily.

"Right," said Mr. Plod. "Noddy—how much do you charge when anyone borrows your car?" "Fifty pence a day," said Noddy. So Gobby is having to pay a lot of money.

And, dear me, what a lot of spankings are waiting for him! Who's that hiding behind a tree with a great big slipper in her paw? It's Mrs. Long-Ears Bunny. Look out, Gobby!

NODDY AND THE MOON

ONCE, when Noddy was going back home at night in his little car, a toy duck called out to him. She was on the banks of a little pond, and she was most upset.

"Noddy! Come here! Something queer has happened."

Noddy stopped his car and got out. He went over to the pond where the toy duck was. She pointed with one of her wings into the water.

"Look, Noddy, look! The moon has fallen into my pond!"

Noddy looked. Sure enough there was the moon shining up at him out of the pond. What a very peculiar thing!

"What are we to do?" said the duck. "The moon can't stay there. How can I swim in a pond when the moon is in it? Noddy, think what to do."

Noddy thought so hard that the bell on the end of his hat tinkled loudly. Then he nodded his head and the bell tinkled again.

"I know what to do, duck. I'll get a net and catch the moon. Then you can swim safely on the pond again."

"There's a net in that little shed," said the duck, so Noddy went to fetch it. Then he put into the pond and fished and fished for the moon.

But he couldn't catch it. He kept thinking he had got it, and then, when he lifted his net out of the water, the moon still lay in the pond, shining brightly.

"The moon is very tiresome," said Noddy. He looked fiercely at it. "Moon, let me catch you! You might drown in this pond. Now, come into my net and be sensible!"

But the moon swam in the pond and wouldn't be caught. Then there came the sound of footsteps, and Noddy looked round. It was Mr. Plod, the policeman.

"What do you think you are doing, fishing in the duck-pond in the middle of the night?" said Mr. Plod.

"I'm fishing for the moon," said Noddy. "Look, it has fallen into the pond, Mr. Plod. See if *you* can catch it!"

Mr. Plod began to laugh. He held his sides and he roared so loudly that the duck was alarmed and began to quack in fright.

"Ha, ha, ha!"

"Quack, quack, quack!"

"HO, HO, HO!"

"QUACK, QUACK, QUACK!"

Noddy was cross. He nearly threw the net at Mr. Plod, but he just didn't. "What's the matter with you, Mr. Plod?" he said.

"Oh, Noddy, look up into the sky!" laughed big Mr. Plod. "Tell me what you see there."

So Noddy looked, and so did the duck. And there was the big round moon sailing merrily among the clouds, shining brightly. It seemed to laugh at Noddy.

"But it's in the pond, too!" said Noddy. "I see it!"

"You look in all the ponds you pass on the way home," said Mr. Plod. "There will be a moon in every one—but not the *real* moon, Noddy. Oh, what a little silly you are!"

So Noddy and the duck went together and looked into all the ponds they passed. And will you believe it, a moon shone in every one.

Noddy still doesn't know why. Do you?

MR. PLOD BEGAN TO LAUGH. HE HELD HIS
SIDES AND ROARED AND ROARED.

I REALLY LOVE A RAINY DAY

"I really love a rainy day,
With puddles in the street,
And raindrops bumping on my nose,
And splishy-splashy feet!
I wish I was a little duck
That didn't wear a mac,
I'd like to feel the raindrops run
All down my feathery back!"

BIG-EARS' UMBRELLA

NOW one day Noddy took little Tessie Bear to have tea with Big-Ears, because Big-Ears was very fond of her. When it was time to take her home again, it was raining.

"It's *pouring!*" said Noddy in dismay. "Oh, Tessie, you'll get so wet in my car. I *wish* I'd brought my umbrella. Big-Ears, will you lend me yours?"

"No," said Big-Ears. "Every time I lend it to you, you forget to bring it back. I told you I wouldn't lend it to you any more, and I meant it."

"But Big-Ears—it's for little Tessie Bear," said Noddy. "Her new hat will be spoilt. She'll get a cold. She will shiver and shake and . . ."

"All right, all right, I'll lend it to you," said Big-Ears. "But *really* I'm lending it to Tessie. And you're to bring it back *tomorrow*, Noddy. If you don't I shall take the bell off your cap and sew it on mine—just to teach you that I mean what I say."

"Oh thank you, Big-Ears, you *are* kind to lend us your umbrella," said Noddy and ran to the corner where it stood. "It's such a lovely big one, it will cover us both. *You* can hold it while I drive, Tessie, can't you?"

"Oh yes," said Tessie. "What a beauty, isn't it—so big —and what a lovely colour!"

Soon they were out in the little car and Noddy put up the big umbrella. It sheltered both of them from the pouring rain. "Now you hold the handle, Tessie," said Noddy. "And I'll drive."

Away they went, quite slowly, the big umbrella over them. Mr. Jumbo and Mr. Wobbly-Man laughed to see them, as they passed by them in Toy Village.

Noddy took Tessie safely home—and by that time the rain had stopped, so they could close the umbrella. "Goodbye, Noddy," said Tessie. "I had a lovely time—and please, Noddy—you *will* remember to take back the umbrella to Big-Ears tomorrow, won't you? Promise?"

"I promise," said Noddy, and away he went, the umbrella beside him on the seat. He took it indoors with him when he got home, determined not to forget it next day. He stood it beside him while he had his supper.

"I'm not going to let you out of my sight!" he said. "You stand there, umbrella—and when I go to bed, you're going to go too, so that nobody can steal you in the night!"

It was funny to see the umbrella lying beside Noddy in

bed, its handle sticking out from under the clothes like a head. Noddy found it rather uncomfortable when he turned over in the middle of the night.

"What's this?" he said. "Oh it's you, umbrella. Move up a bit. You're dreadfully hard and long."

Noddy stood it beside his breakfast table next morning, and he took it to the garage with him when he went to clean his car. He stood it close beside him so that he should keep seeing it. That would remind him that he MUST keep his promise and take it back to Big-Ears.

At last his car was shining and clean. Noddy washed his hands and got into the driving seat. He put the umbrella beside him in the passenger's seat, and there it was, trying to look like a proper passenger!

"Now we'll go to Big-Ears," said Noddy. "And NOTHING will stop me from delivering you safely, umbrella. You'll soon be standing in your own little corner of Toadstool House."

But something did stop him! Halfway through the village who should come galloping across the road in front of the car but Bumpy, the toy dog! Noddy put on his brakes and just stopped in time.

"You silly dog, Bumpy!" he shouted crossly. "What do you mean by prancing about in front of my car like that? I might have run you over!"

"Wuffy-wuff!" said Bumpy joyfully, and ran up to Noddy and gave him an enormous lick on his nose.

"DON'T!" said Noddy. "Why are you so licky? *I* don't go round licking everyone!"

"Wuff!" said Bumpy, and leapt into the seat beside Noddy. Noddy pushed him out at once.

"NO!" he said. "Can't you see I've got Big-Ears' umbrella there? I'm taking it back to him because he lent it to me—and I *promised* he should have it today. I'm not taking anyone in my car till he's got it back."

Bumpy jumped into the car again—and oh dear,

Noddy gave him such a smack that he jumped out at once, put his tail down and looked very miserable indeed. "Wuff!" he said, in a very, very small voice.

Noddy started off again—and then he stopped. Something was wrong with one of his tyres—what was it? He jumped out to see.

"Oh! I've got a big stone stuck in my back tyre!" he said. "I must get it out before it makes a hole. But oh dear—what shall I get it out with? Oh—*I* know—I'll poke it out with Big-Ears' umbrella! Just the thing!"

So he got Big-Ears' umbrella and poked out the big stone. Bumpy came to watch, his tail down. But Noddy was still cross with him.

"Go away! You're a nuisance. If you lick my nose again you'll get another smack, Bumpy Dog!" Then he got into his car and drove away at top speed. Aha! That was the way to treat the Bumpy Dog if he made a nuisance of himself!

The Bumpy Dog sat down sorrowfully on the pave-

ment. He did like Noddy so much and he couldn't *bear* being smacked. Then he suddenly saw something lying on the pavement.

Will you believe it, it was Big-Ears' umbrella! Yes—Noddy had forgotten to put it back into his car again. He had driven off without it. The Bumpy Dog looked and looked at it. What had Noddy said? He had said he was taking it back to Big-Ears—and now he had forgotten it!

Bumpy made up his mind at once. He would race after Noddy with it, and give it to him. Then perhaps he wouldn't be cross with him any more. So away he trotted, with the big umbrella in his mouth.

Noddy was a long way ahead. He had reach Big-Ears' house and Big-Ears came to meet him. "Well, Noddy—so you've come to give me back my umbrella?" he said, pleased.

"Yes," said Noddy, and looked for it on the seat beside him. But it wasn't there!

"Oh! I left it behind on the pavement in Toy Village!" he said. "Goodness me, someone may have taken it by now! Oh Big-Ears, I did mean to bring it. I'll go straight back and . . ."

"There! You've forgotten it *again*!" said Big-Ears, really cross—and oh dear, he took a pair of scissors from

his pocket and snipped off the bell on the top of Noddy's hat! "Now it's *my* bell—and I shall sew it on *my* hat!"

Noddy began to wail. "No, no—I tell you I was *bringing* your umbrella here, I really was, Big-Ears. Please let me have my bell. Big-Ears, I tell you. . . ."

But Big-Ears had gone into his house to sew the bell on *his* hat. Oh dear! But wait a minute, who was this panting up the woodland path?

"It's Bumpy!" cried Noddy. "And oh, he's got the umbrella! You saw I'd left it behind, Bumpy—and though I'd smacked you and been cross, you still wanted to help me. Bumpy, I love you, I think you're very, very kind."

And he jumped out of his car, and ran to hug Bumpy very hard indeed. Bumpy was so pleased. Then Noddy went to give Big-Ears the umbrella.

"Here it is—you're *not* to sew my bell on your hat!" he cried, and he took away his little bell at once. Big-Ears laughed.

"All right. I don't know how you managed to find my umbrella so quickly—but you're only just in time to have back your bell. Shall I sew it on your hat for you?"

"No. I'm lending it to someone else for the day," said

Noddy. And what do you suppose he did? He let the Bumpy Dog sit beside him in the car, and he drove to the market and bought a blue ribbon for him. Then he threaded the bell on to the ribbon and hung it round Bumpy's neck. It went jingle-jingle-jing all the time.

Bumpy was so proud and pleased that he really didn't know what to do! He galloped and pranced and bounded and skipped till Noddy felt quite dizzy.

"Bring it back tomorrow," he said to Bumpy. "But now you can go and show it to little Tessie Bear. She *will* be so surprised!"

So off went Bumpy, with a jingle-jingle-jing. Wasn't it nice of Noddy to think of such a treat for him?

BIG-EARS' CAT GETS INTO TROUBLE

One morning Noddy was on his way to see Big-Ears, when he saw someone waving to him from the pavement. "Oh—it's little Tessie Bear!" he thought. "Good! I'll take her for a ride in my car. Hey, Tessie—jump in!"

Tessie was very pleased. "I hope you aren't very busy, Noddy," she said. "Have you many jobs to do?"

"No, I was going to see Big-Ears," said Noddy, and away they went at top speed through the wood.

Big-Ears was very pleased to see little Tessie Bear. He shook hands with her, and said he liked the bow under her chin.

"Noddy—where's my shopping?" he said. "And did you remember to bring back my umbrella that I lent you?"

"Oh *dear!*" said Noddy, and took an empty basket from his car. "I *meant* to fetch your shopping, Big-Ears. And I *meant* to bring your umbrella. I'm very sorry!" But Big-Ears was cross, and wouldn't ask Noddy into his house.

"I'd got cakes and lemonade ready for you, but you don't deserve any now," he said. "Please go away."

So Noddy drove sadly away with Tessie Bear and the empty basket. "Nasty old Big-Ears!" said Noddy.

"He *was* cross," said Tessie. "Oh Noddy—what's that loud noise in the wood? Stop a minute, please."

So they stopped—and Tessie soon found out what was making the noise. "Look," she said, "there's a cat . . .

"Right at the top of that tree. It can't get down, poor thing." Noddy looked. "Gracious!" he said. "It's Big-Ears' cat!"

"Well—he was so horrid to me just now that I won't bother about his silly cat." And he got back into the car.

Little Tessie Bear was shocked. "Oh *Noddy*! The poor frightened cat! Well—I'm going to stay and try to help it."

"I'll stay, too," said Noddy. "I didn't *mean* what I said. I like Big-Ears' cat. I'll climb up and get it. Here goes. . . ."

Noddy climbed right up to the very top of the tree—but although the cat miaowed loudly, it wouldn't go down.

"It's afraid," called down Noddy. "What can we do, Tessie?" "I'll throw up the basket," said Tessie. . . .

"Then you can put the cat into it and climb down." So she threw up the basket, and Noddy put the cat into it.

But oh dear—he couldn't climb down with the heavy cat in the basket, because he needed both hands to climb with!

He nearly fell down himself. Whatever was he to do? Then he scrambled down the tree quickly. . . .

"I've a good idea, Tessie," he said. "I've left the cat safely up there in the basket, look, but what we want is. . . .

"Some rope or something to tie to it so that I can gently let the basket down to the ground. Now, let's think." "Let's tie your shoe-laces together—and your scarf—and my belt!" said Tessie. "They will make a fine rope."

So Noddy untied his shoe laces and took off his scarf, and Tessie gave him her belt, and now see. . . .

They are all tied together into a fine rope! Up to the tree goes Noddy again, and now he ties the queer rope. . . .

To the handle of the basket. The cat miaowed. "It's all right," said Noddy. "I'm going to let you down the tree. . . .

Like this—very gently. Don't bump against the branches. Hold tight, cat. Tessie, it's coming down, be ready!"

The basket swung slowly down the tree on the strange rope. Now Tessie is reaching out her arms for it.

And she caught the basket safely in her arms! The cat jumped down, mewing loudly. It was very pleased.

And then who should come up but Big-Ears! How surprised he was to see what Tessie and Noddy were doing!

"Your cat was up the tree and couldn't get down," said Tessie. "So we made a rope and Noddy climbed up."

"You're very very kind—especially as I was cross with you," said Big-Ears, picking up his cat. "You're to come back with me this very minute, and have those cakes and lemonade. Come along!"

So they all went back to Big-Ears' house in the car, though it was a bit of a squash because the cat came, too.

And now what a feast they are having. You can hardly see Noddy because the cat *will* sit on his knee!

135

NODDY'S LUDO GAME

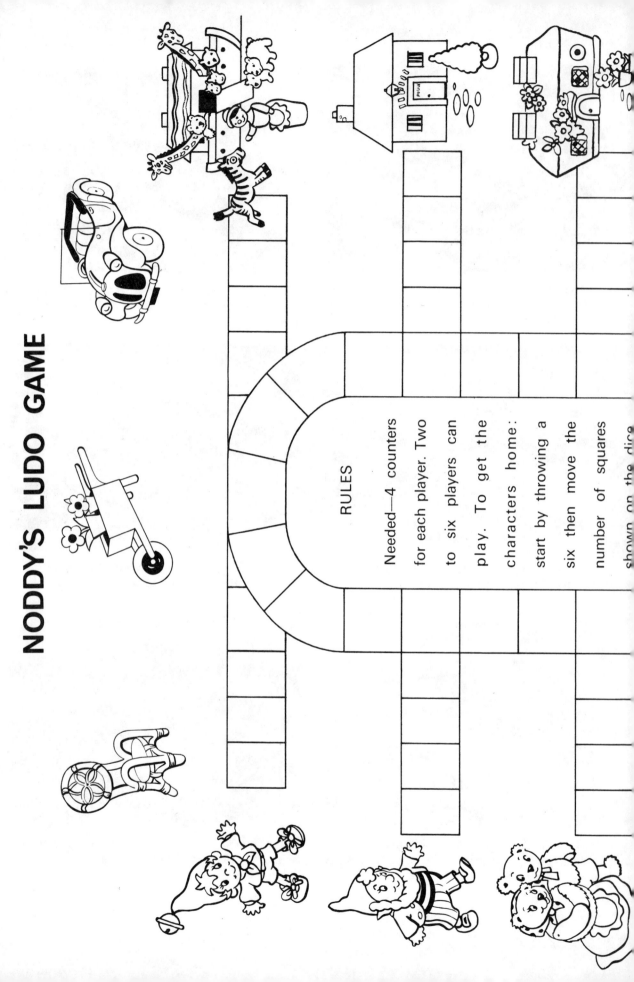

RULES

Needed—4 counters for each player. Two to six players can play. To get the characters home: start by throwing a six then move the number of squares shown on the dice

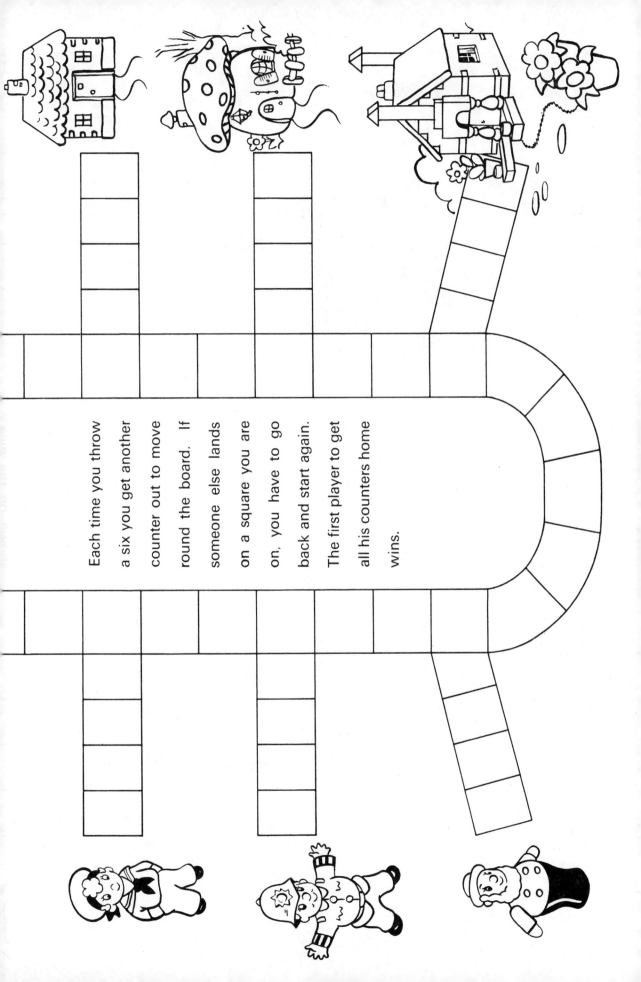

Each time you throw a six you get another counter out to move round the board. If someone else lands on a square you are on, you have to go back and start again. The first player to get all his counters home wins.

NODDY AND THE HORSE

ONE morning Mr. Tubby Bear came knocking at Noddy's door. Noddy was just finishing his breakfast. "Come in!" he called.

Mr. Tubby walked in. He only lived next door, so he hadn't come far. He looked rather worried.

"Noddy," he said, "Mrs. Tubby has caught a bad cold. I've got to go and make a call in the next village, so I shall *have* to leave her by herself this morning. Do you think you would mind popping in and out to see if she wants anything?"

"Oh, I'd *love* to," said Noddy at once. He was very fond of kind Mrs. Tubby Bear. "Yes, of course I'll pop in and out. I'll do as much popping as you want me to."

"Mrs. Tubby was up very early this morning," said Mr. Tubby, "and so she has done most of her work—but now she has gone to bed because her cold is so bad. She has done all the washing, and all the sweeping, but not the dusting."

"I'll do that," said Noddy. "I like dusting. I'll be very very careful not to break anything."

"Thank you, little Noddy," said Mr. Tubby. "Well, I'll go now. I'll be back by dinner-time."

Off he went. Noddy tidied his tiny house, went to tell his car he wouldn't want it that morning, and then went to Mrs. Tubby Bear's house next door. He went in and called up the stairs.

"Are you there, Mrs. Tubby? Shall I come up?"

"Yes, Noddy," called Mrs. Tubby. "Make a cup of cocoa for yourself and bring me up some hot milk, there's a dear little fellow!"

Noddy soon had it ready and he carried it up. Then he said he would do the dusting. He said he would wash up the breakfast things, too, because Mr. Tubby Bear hadn't had time to do them.

How busy he was! He dusted every room well, but he forgot that he had done the parlour, so he dusted it all over again, wondering why it looked so clean.

He washed up the breakfast things, and then he heard Mrs. Tubby's voice again.

"Oh, Noddy—it's raining hard. Will you go and bring in the horse for me?"

Noddy was surprised. The horse? Dear me, had Mr. Tubby got a *horse?* Well, well—why had he never told him?

He looked into the garden. It certainly was raining hard. He saw the washing on the line—and he saw a clothes-horse out there, too, with little tea-cloths and Mr. Tubby's collars and hankies on it. Oughtn't he to bring in the washing?

He called to Mrs. Tubby: "Shall I take the washing off the line?"

"No, that doesn't matter. The rain will do it good," said Mrs. Tubby. "But please bring the horse in out of the rain. Go and fetch it now."

Noddy stared out of the window. He didn't know that Mrs. Tubby meant the clothes-horse that stood out in the garden with small things on it. He thought she meant a proper horse.

And then he saw a dear little toy horse in the field at the back of the garden. Ah—that must be the horse that Mrs. Tubby meant.

"It's funny she wants it brought into the house," thought Noddy. "*I* don't think it minds the rain. And, dear me, what a noise it will make in this little kitchen."

Still, out he went to catch the horse. He climbed over the wall and ran to it. It ran away. Noddy ran after it, getting wetter and wetter in the rain. He got quite cross with the horse!

But at last he caught it and led it through the gate, into the garden, and up to the kitchen door. The horse didn't want to go indoors. Noddy had to push it in.

It didn't like the kitchen and began to gallop round it, knocking down a chair and a table.

Mrs. Tubby Bear heard all this noise in surprise. Good gracious! Was that Noddy racing round the kitchen in big cloppity-clop boots? What *was* he doing?

"Hrrrrrrumph!" said the horse suddenly, and Noddy almost jumped out of his skin. Mrs. Tubby Bear nearly fell out of bed. What a noise! Whatever was happening?

"Noddy! What are you doing?" she called.

"I've just brought the horse in, but it won't stand still. It keeps galloping about," called Noddy, quite angry with the horse.

Mrs. Tubby Bear lay and imagined her clothes-horse galloping round and round the kitchen. How peculiar! She decided to get up and find out what really was going on. So up she got and was just going down the stairs when she met the horse rushing up with Noddy after it.

"Oh my!" said poor Mrs. Tubby and ran back into her bedroom. "A horse! A real horse! What *can* Noddy be thinking of?"

Very luckily Mr. Tubby Bear came back at that very moment. He met the horse coming downstairs, and could hardly believe his eyes. He gave it a hard smack and sent it out into the garden.

"Oh, it mustn't go out in the rain!" wailed Noddy. "Mrs. Tubby wanted the horse brought indoors."

Mr. Tubby Bear stared. Then he laughed so loudly that Noddy jumped. "She meant the clothes-horse, silly. Didn't you know that that was a clothes-horse standing out there, with my collars and hankies on?"

"No. No, I didn't," said Noddy, and he burst into tears. "Oh dear—and I went and fetched a proper horse, Mr. Tubby. Don't be cross with me."

"I won't," said Mr. Tubby. "I can see what a lot of work you have done for me, Noddy. Cheer up! You may be a silly goose, but you're a nice little Noddy. Cheer up!"

So Noddy cheered up till the horse came and looked in at the window. Oh dear—go away, horse! Noddy really doesn't want to see you any more!

HURRAH FOR MISS RAP

"Hurrah for Miss Rap,
She is perfectly sweet,
From the hair on her head
To the toes on her feet.
She teaches us writing,
She teaches us sums,

And everyone's happy
Whenever she comes!
Hurrah for Miss Rap,
We've just heard her say,
'You've done your work well,
Now go out to play!'"

NODDY'S CAR RUNS AWAY

Here comes little Noddy in his car, a smile on his face as usual. Hallo, little Noddy! Ah! I thought he would stop at an ice-cream shop. Noddy likes ice-creams as much as you do!

Out he gets, and, because the shop is on the top of a steep hill, he is careful to put on his brakes.

Oh, what an enormous ice-cream, Noddy! You will never, never eat all that! Is it a very nice one?

Noddy is enjoying his ice-cream so much that he doesn't see two naughty little bears peeping in at the door.

"He's not looking," one says to the other. "Let's get into his car. Quick!"

So here are the two bad bears in Noddy's car, pretending to drive it. Oh dear—one takes off the brakes. . . .

And because the car is on the top of a hill, it begins to run down it. The bears are very frightened.

"Quick, jump out!" says one, and out they both jump, look! They land in the road with a bump.

But the little car goes on and on down the hill at top speed. Look out, policeman!

There—the car has run right into him and knocked him over. Away goes his helmet into the air!

On goes the car. Mind that barrow of oranges! Don't bump into it, you silly little car!

But it has, look! Oh dear me, what a lot of oranges are rolling down the hill. How angry the barrow-man is!

On goes the car again. It can't stop. And now here comes a load of logs on a wooden lorry. . . .

Bang! Biff! The car goes into the lorry and it falls over. And now there are logs rolling down the hill as well as oranges! "Stop that car, stop it!" everybody yells. "Hey, you skittles, look out! You'll be knocked down!"

The skittles were walking up the hill in a row. Crash! The little car ran right into them. Down they went.

"They're skittles. They're used to being knocked over!" said big Mr. Jumbo. "Look at them rolling away."

147

Well, really, it was getting quite difficult for people to walk up the hill, what with oranges, logs and skittles rolling down!

And now, what is little Noddy doing while his car is running away? He has finished his ice, and he is paying his bill.

Now he is outside. Dear me—where is his car? "Where's it gone?" wails Noddy. "Where is my dear little car?" "It's run down the hill," said a golly, pointing. "Two little bears were in it. It went down the hill, Noddy!"

Now here goes little Noddy down the hill, too! Oh dear—he sees the upset barrow and the lorry—and there are the skittles, too!

Where do you think his car is? At the bottom of the hill is a big pond—and the car ran right into it, splash!

Everyone is surprised to see a car run into the pond. The policeman is cross. The barrow-man is cross.

The skittles are VERY cross, and so is the man who drove the lorry of logs. "Where's the owner of this car?" they shout.

"Oh dear, oh dear—I'm the owner," says little Noddy. "I was just having an ice-cream. Oh, my poor little car!"

"Gurgle-gurgle!" said the car, trying to hoot under the water. Noddy can't bear it. He jumps into the water. . . .

But he can't pull out the car. Somebody throws him a rope. "Tie the rope to the car! Then it will be easier to pull!"

But still Noddy couldn't pull it—and now look who's helping! Good old Mr. Jumbo had got hold of the rope. Pull, Jumbo, pull!

And up comes the car with a run, dripping wet and shivering! Hurrah! But up comes the policeman too, with a frown.

"I'm afraid you'll have to come with me," he says to Noddy. "Your car has done a lot of damage."

"I can tell you who's to blame," said Mr. Jumbo. "It was those two bad bears over there, look—catch them, somebody!"

So the bears were caught, and the policeman is taking them away to give them a very good telling off.

And Noddy helped to pick up the oranges and logs, and told the skittles to come to tea with him to make up for their fright.

And there he goes back home again, to dry his little car and comfort it. "Parp-parp!" says the car happily. "I'll soon be all right again. Parp-parp!"

SAILOR DOLL'S PARTY

ONE night Mr. Sailor Doll gave a party in his little house. Dear me, what a party it was! There was so much noise that Mrs. Minnie Monkey, who lived next door, came out to complain.

But nobody took any notice of her at all. Then some more of Mr. Sailor Doll's friends came along, and soon there was not enough room in his house to dance or play games.

"Let's go into the garden," said one of the Sailor Doll's friends, Mr. Hearty. "It's nice and big. We'll have room there to dance the horn-pipe."

So they went into the garden—but, of course, it was too dark to dance.

"We want a few lamp-posts," said Mr. Hearty, "let's go and get some."

But just as Mr. Sailor and his friends were setting off to get some lamp-posts, who should come along in his car, but little Noddy!

"We'll get *him* to fetch some," said the Sailor Doll. "It will save us the bother of carrying them. He can easily lay them across his car and bring three or four at a time."

"But he'll be afraid of Mr. Plod the policeman coming after him, if he takes away the lamp-posts from the corners," said Mr. Hearty.

The Sailor Doll laughed —he was in a very naughty mood that night.

"We'll tell Noddy that Mr. Plod has said he can bring all the  lamp-posts here," he said. He went into the road and stopped Noddy's car.

"Noddy!" he said, "there's a message for you from Mr. Plod."

"Oh dear—have I done anything wrong?" said Noddy.

"No. It's just to say that you are to go and collect as

many lamp-posts
as you can, and
bring them here,"
said Mr. Sailor
Doll.

"*Really?*" said
Noddy, aston-
ished. "All right.
I'll go and get a
few now. What
do you want them
for?"

"To light my
garden for a dance," said Mr. Sailor Doll, and that made
Noddy feel more surprised than ever. Fancy Mr. Plod
saying that the Sailor Doll could have all the village
lamp-posts in his garden for a dance!

Off he went. He came to a lamp-post, got out, lifted it
up and laid it across his car. Then he took the second

lamp-post he saw, and the
third and the fourth. He drove
back to Mr. Sailor Doll's with
them, and soon the tall lamp-
posts were lighting up his
garden.

Soon Noddy had taken half
the lamp-posts to Mr. Sailor
Doll's garden. When Mr. Plod
set out that evening, he was MOST astonished to find

hardly any lamp-posts in the streets.

"I must be dreaming!" he said, staring at this corner and that. "WHERE are all the lamp-posts? What a very, very peculiar thing!"

He thought it was even more peculiar when he went round a corner and suddenly saw a blaze of light in Mr. Sailor Doll's garden!

"Goodness gracious! All the lamp-posts are *there*!" said

Mr. Plod, and he rubbed his eyes. "I certainly MUST be in a dream. Hallo—here's little Noddy in his car. Whatever is he carrying in it—three lamp-posts!"

Noddy drove by and beamed at the astonished policeman. "Hallo, Mr. Plod!" he said. "I got your message all right—and I'm taking as many lamp-posts as I can to Mr. Sailor Doll's garden, as you said. Can I give you a lift? There's just room."

Mr. Plod stared at little Noddy. Yes, this must certainly be a dream. Noddy would certainly never, never come and tell him things like this if he were awake. He got into the car.

"I suppose you are going to the party too," said little Noddy, driving up to Sailor Doll's house. "It's a very, very good one. I hope you enjoy it, Mr. Plod."

MR. PLOD JOINED THE PARTY AND SANG AND DANCED

Well, Mr. Plod thought he might as well join the party and have a good time, because he still thought it was a dream. So to Mr. Sailor Doll's great surprise, Mr. Plod came smiling in at the gate and joined the party. He sang and he danced, and everyone enjoyed themselves thoroughly, Noddy too.

"Shall I take the lamp-posts back, Mr. Plod?" asked Noddy, at the end of the party.

"Oh, no!" said Mr. Plod. "This is only a dream, little Noddy. It's quite likely that the lamp-posts will take themselves back, you know. It's quite a *jolly* dream, isn't it?"

"*I* didn't know it was a dream," said Noddy, surprised. "Well, I'm going home to bed. Can I give you a lift?"

Mr. Plod got sleepily into Noddy's car, and they drove off. Noddy stopped outside the police station and Mr. Plod got out. "See you tomorrow morning when I'm awake, little Noddy," he said and went indoors. Noddy was really very puzzled. "*I'm* not in a dream, so how can *he* be?'' he said. ''Oh well—I'm glad I haven't got to take all those lamp-posts back tonight!''

In the morning, what a to-do there was! Everyone came knocking at Mr. Plod's door, complaining that all the village lamp-posts were standing in Sailor Doll's garden.

''WHO has taken them there, Mr. Plod?'' said Sally Skittle.

''Find out and give him a spanking!'' said Miss Fluffy Cat.

But little Noddy is quite safe. Mr. Plod simply doesn't dare to tell tales of him.

''Oh dear!'' he groans, ''so it *wasn't* a dream after all— and I went to that party, and danced the horn-pipe under those shining lamp-posts. *What* would people say if they knew?''

Poor Mr. Plod. He really is very upset about it!